SHIVAJI AND THE MYSTERY OF THE BHAVANI SWORD

SHIVAJI AND THE MYSTERY OF THE BHAVANI SWORD

SHRADDHA SAHI

An imprint of
Srishti Publishers & Distributors

Srishti Publishers & Distributors
A unit of AJR Publishing LLP
212A, Peacock Lane
Shahpur Jat, New Delhi – 110 049

editorial@srishtipublishers.com

First Published by Launchpad,
An imprint of Srishti Publishers & Distributors in 2026

10 9 8 7 6 5 4 3 2 1

Printed and bound in India.

For Aai and Baba

Acknowledgements

From the first time I read about Shivaji Maharaj in third standard history, to the many detailed biographies I used to fact-check while writing this book, each work added to my awe and admiration for this great Maratha King. Thank you to all the men and women who devoted so much love and attention to bringing to life a gigantic personality who is nothing short of God for most Maharashtrians.

This book has had a long and strange journey from the time travel adventure it first set out to be, when the Naikwadi children met Tanaji. The man instrumental in helping me proudly present it to the world is my sometimes morale-boosting, sometimes exasperated, always (in the end) right literary agent of The Book Bakers, Suhail Mathur. He always knows what will work, and lives and breathes each of his authors' books. Every post, podcast and interview with him will teach you more than any course on being a writer! Thank you, Suhail, from the bottom of my heart.

My fellow writers from The Book Bakers group have always encouraged loudly, suggested softly and reviewed brilliantly. Thank you, Vani, Rrashima, Padmini, Bhaswar *da*, Kavya, Sushama, Sonia, Aparna, Debeshi, Sudesna, Nitya, Souvik, Monica and Nilshree for your support!

The people behind the scenes play the biggest role of all. A huge debt of gratitude to Ma, Didi, Vikram, and my sunshine – Anshul.

Sharwin and Shanaya – you are my brand ambassadors, and I hope you'll like this one too!

Roopali, Vaibhavi, Poorva, Sameer, Sapna, Nandini, Snehala, Kaustubh – thank you for your friendship and support.

A big shout out to my publisher at Srishti – Arup Bose and his talented team for all the hard work and love they gave to the book.

Meet the Naikwadi Gang

Prajakta Naik: Thirteen-year-old firebrand who runs faster than the boys in her village, and bonds with animals, almost seeming to read their minds. Unusually progressive for her time, she wants to follow in her father's footsteps and become a healer.

Sarjya Naik: Eleven-year-old bundle of mischief who idolizes Shivaji Raje. Food is a big priority and one of the few ways you can get him to sit still. He acts first and thinks later, but has an uncanny ability to stumble across interesting stuff. His dog, Kaloo, is his faithful shadow.

Ganya: Sarjya's best friend and co-conspirator. His friends call him a human peacock for his garish dress sense. Ganya excels at mimicry – of animals and people, and is supremely self-confident; though of late, he's become touchy and gone into his shell.

Sopan: The blacksmith's son is a sensitive, poetic dreamer who's growing up to be a tall, strapping lad. He's always the first to lend a helping hand, and is remarkably mature for his age. He loves learning all about weapons and hopes to help design some of his own.

Prologue

May, 1674
The King's Chambers, Raigad

The blood-red ruby dazzled in the glow of the setting sun. It blinked and flashed malevolently at the man, as if Goddess Bhavani herself was glaring at him with enraged eyes. His heartbeat pounded in his ears, much like the beating drums that announced Shivaji's decrees. *Stop being a superstitious fool*! Sweating, he covered the ruby with his long fingers so he couldn't see it looking at him, just in case there was any truth to all the myths. Quickly using his dagger to prise out the ruby, he then did the same for the gigantic emerald.

Dash it! The jewels nearly slipped from his trembling fingers. He had been warned the sword was heavy, but he had thought if that diminutive King of theirs could lift it, so could he. The man was aware of how little time he had, and what would happen if they caught him. Tales of prisoners being thrown off Takmak Tok were legendary; now he'd get to experience it for himself if he failed in this task.

He strained to breathe… had the air around him suddenly become thinner? The man placed his hand over his chest, willing the thudding inside to slow. After all, it wasn't the first time he had stolen stuff – he never could resist shiny, expensive things – but this was on a whole other level. Unbidden, memories of the woman he had called mother arose; how she'd look at his growing collection of stolen baubles and laugh, calling him a magpie. She had quickly realized the light-fingered child could earn his keep that way, but in all those years, she never showed love, kindness, or approval for his 'skills'. He wondered for the millionth time if he would have been better off without her.

Forget all that now and focus, he mopped the sweat dripping into his eyes and dried his palms on his kurta before shifting his attention back to the massive sword. If he wasn't careful enough, the lethal blade would slice through his palms in a flash, just like Shivaji had finished off so many of his enemies. The man exhaled slowly, then moved on to the diamonds; they weren't necessary – the giant had told him to get only the ruby and the emerald. But he just couldn't help himself… one, two, three… *Hurry, hurry, I can hear footsteps!* Eleven small diamonds were all he had time for… should be enough to disfigure the impressive hilt, and ensure that anyone who saw it would notice.

There was just enough time to put the sword back on the rack. The man was still breathing heavily as he gave the famous weapon one last look. They said it was a divine blessing from the Goddess; he snorted – that blade had brought about so many deaths… But he wasn't going to allow himself to think about that or that heavy fog of grief would engulf him again.

Oh no, the scabbard! No time to put it in its place now; he shoved it under the low bed, and then palpated his way to the hiding place for the jewels. Time was running out! Thank God they had rehearsed his movements – who knew fear could make his usually nimble fingers feel so clumsy!

The man forced himself to breathe normally – if he continued gasping like this, the truth would be out in no time. There, it was done! He dashed back to where he was expected to be, then tucked a few stray strands of greying hair behind his ears, and patted his face dry. He was ready to act like a snivelling, deferential subject again!

Chapter 1

September, 1671 (3 Years Prior)
Naikwadi, near Pune

The billowing grey cloud of dust settled as the small troop of Mughal riders thundered past the crouching boy. In the dense bushes below the small trail, Sarjya waited until the forest was silent, and then a bit more, till the birds began to twitter again. Finally, he stood up to unclench his fist and loosen his deathly grip on the small rock he had picked up to throw at the lead rider. He watched the stone roll away, the sweaty imprint of his palm still on it, and marvelled at his own self-control. Prajakta *Tai* would be surprised and proud, he beamed; she was always on his case about being too impulsive. He could almost see her there, her oiled plaits flying around as she shook her head at him and scolded, 'You always jump first and think later!'

Sarjya stuck out his tongue at this vision of his always sensible sister and dusted off the bits of grass and twigs from his *kurta*. He had dived into the bushes when Sundari and the other grazing cows had hinted of the approaching riders. Sarjya knew that his excellent aim would have knocked the menacing-looking soldier right off his horse. But then what? The rest of the men would have hauled him off to God knows where, and then... he shuddered. Naikwadi had not been troubled by Aurangzeb's troops for some months now; this little stray group must have just been passing by on their way to terrorize some other village. It was a good thing he had left them alone; otherwise, like an angry swarm of bees, they would have followed him back to his village.

Nine-year-old Sarjya leapt onto his favourite cow's back and whispered, "Look, Sundari, how sensible I have become! I'm grown up now, nearly a man. In a few years, Raje himself will beg me to join his army!" As he clicked his tongue and nudged the herd to turn for home, he thought about the soldiers who had ridden past – their scarily impressive black uniforms, and how they sat up in their saddles. But Shivaji Raje's soldiers were much more regal and better trained, the loyal thought arose. He would become one of them soon... Sarjya Naik, *Subhedar* of the most daring division of Shivaji's troops! He would look so impressive mounted on his white steed – all the village girls would line up to admire him, and the boys would secretly wish to be like him!

Sarjya let out a whoop and urged Sundari to move faster. "Come on, you are my trusted horse, and we are heading to the Mughal camp to strike the fear of God into them! *Har Har Mahadev!*" He dug his heels into the cow's side, drawing a loud protesting moo from her. Sundari was used to her master's crazy antics, but the calf behind her wasn't. Spooked by the maniacal yelling and the deafening whoops emanating from Sarjya, the poor thing bolted. The ripple effect caused the herd to bump into each other, and the galloping Sundari to stumble. Sarjya was thrown off the cow at high speed into a deep, muddy ditch. The last thought that flashed across his mind before he blacked out was, *Tai will be so mad!*

Chapter 2

"Aah!"

"Stop moving, you naughty child!" Baba growled. His exhausted face lit up with the smallest of smiles to reassure his son that he wasn't furious at his behaviour – well, not much.

"Sarjya!" Prajakta rushed to her brother's side and said, "You're finally awake, you crazy boy!"

Crazy? Sarjya bristled. "I'm not…," his words died at the look on Baba's face.

"If Kaloo had not raced home and dragged your sister to the forest, only *Aai Bhavani* knows how many hours you would have lain there, bloodied and with a broken leg," Baba said.

"B... broken?" Sarjya looked down at his bandaged leg and, as if reminded, his body began to throb alarmingly. "*Aah,* it hurts! Make it stop!" he began to howl.

"Shh, my boy, don't move. Drink this and lie down quietly. It'll help with the pain," Baba said, pressing a small bowl of foul-smelling green stuff into his hands.

The sight of the *kaadha* made Sarjya gag, but he knew Baba's remedies were highly effective and famous even two villages away.

Prajakta gripped one of her brother's hands tightly and refused to let go. As he supported the bowl with his other hand, Sarjya looked at her pale, grim face, and felt a twinge of remorse. Maybe he hadn't become as sensible as he believed.

Hours later, when he woke again, Aai was by his side with a plate of steaming-hot *varan bhaat*. Sarjya let her feed him, wincing every time he chewed. Even the slightest movement set off a blinding pain in his right leg. Taking shallow breaths, he gingerly let his hand fall to his side. His fingers made contact with soft fur. "Kaloo?" Sarjya looked down into dark, unblinking eyes, and a small head cocked to one side in concern.

"He hasn't left your side since we brought you home," Aai whispered, "maybe now that you are having something, he will also eat. The poor fellow refused all food and just sat there, looking up at your sleeping form and whimpering."

Sarjya pulled the dog closer. "My best friend, you saved me! *Chal,* eat something. I'm fine now." Kaloo looked at his master and woofed; then he licked Sarjya's face and wagged his tail.

Prajakta looked into the dog's soulful eyes and smiled, "He's exhausted being your best friend, he says!"

"Sarjya!" Ganya burst into the room. "I heard you are awake!" He plonked himself down by his best friend's side.

"Owww!" Sarjya screamed. "*Jadya,* move away from my leg!"

The boy's face fell, "Sorry, sorry! Just excited to hear that you are better now. No need to comment on my weight!"

"The pain is making him cranky, Ganya. In fact, you're looking so thin nowadays! Is that a new kurta?" Prajakta watched the hurt in Ganya's eyes give way to his usual bravado, and urged him to have some jaggery laadoos. "Aai just made a fresh lot; she says they will give Sarjya strength to heal faster, especially in this damp weather. You must taste them!"

"Brr," Ganya spoke with his mouth full. "Yes, it's much colder today, Tai. Good thing Kaloo dragged you to the forest. Imagine if Sarjya had lain hidden in the wet grass all night, or if the wolves had smelled his blood!"

Prajakta blanched. "Don't talk rubbish! All the wolves have been killed now." She gave her brother a quick glance, causing him to lower his eyes. He had been really stupid.

***

'Look at her! So tall and still growing!'

'I've told Savitri so many times about my marriageable brother in Wai, but she just gives me a helpless smile. The whole family is weird!'

The voices rose and fell as did Prajakta's heartbeat as she waited for her turn at the village well; this kind of talk had been going on for a year now. Nearly all the girls her age were married, and their mothers would look at Prajakta's parents accusingly, and at her with scorn, *'Too good for our boys, is she?'*

At first, Prajakta smiled at such remarks; then she tried to explain that she was in no hurry to get married because she wanted to become a healer just like Baba, but that only elicited incredulous laughter. In sheer frustration, Prajakta even contemplated telling the Naikwadi villagers that she was becoming an ascetic and renouncing all worldly pleasures, namely marriage, but Baba had frowned on that.

"Maybe we could say you secretly married someone, and he died in battle!" Sarjya came up with that one.

"*Arre,* she will have to shave off her head and wear white clothes!" Aai nearly slapped him.

"It's not that I never want to get married," a red-faced Prajakta mumbled, "just not yet."

Over the next few days, Sarjya was able to sit up for a while without feeling faint, and his appetite returned with a vengeance. The Naikwadi villagers kept sending over delicious food for him, but most of the dishes came from Shaku, who was now in her seventh month of pregnancy, and craved sweets all day.

"Kaku?" Shaku faltered at the door, a strange expression on her face.

"What is it, dear?" Aai rushed to Shaku's side. "Is it the baby? Is it coming early? I told you not to move around so much!"

"No, no, the baby is fine!" she said, biting her lower lip. "I am planning to go to my mother's house in Sangamner next week and stay there for at least six months." Shaku lowered herself to the ground and glanced at Prajakta, hovering around concernedly. "Kaku, can Prajakta come with me?"

Savitri Naik's smile froze. "To Sangamner? I don't… she's too… I'll speak with Prajakta's Baba and let you know, but-"

Prajakta tried to keep from giggling at the combination of horror and panic on her mother's face.

"Do you think she will say yes?" Shaku asked.

"I doubt it! But this is the only way to get away from all the talk of getting me married. Baba knows how I feel, but he's unable to speak up and be the lone voice of reason in the village. They'll all say he's a selfish father who wants his daughter to stay unmarried."

"When you told me you wanted to run away, I thought this plan might at least give you some breathing space."

Prajakta inhaled sharply. "That's if Aai and Baba agree to let me go with you."

The girls turned, and caught Sarjya straining to decipher their whispered conversation, so they hurried to talk of other things.

"So, Sarjya," Shaku asked, "are your eyes better now?"

"*Aga* Shaku Tai, I hurt my leg, not my eyes."

The dimples in Shaku's cheeks deepened as she teased, "But I thought the cows had begun to look like horses to you! Do you think this vision problem also affected your brain, and that's why you suddenly began to think you could ride like a warrior?"

Sarjya scowled at the giggling girls and dropped back onto the mattress, desperately praying for his leg to heal miraculously overnight so he could walk away every time someone reminded him of his brief spell of lunacy.

So much had changed in the past year; the boys hardly had time to frolic like before. Sopan's father, Hanumanta, had passed on most of his duties as the village blacksmith to his son while he devoted all his hours learning how to fashion swords. Shivaji Raje himself had selected Hanumanta as one of the three men sent for training with the Portuguese master swordsmith in Kalyan. Sopan didn't mind the extra chores ac all; it was a matter of immense pride that his father's hands would fashion the very blades the brave Marathas would fight with. Besides, Sopan loved working in the little workshop where he'd sing softly as he worked, sweat pouring down his face.

"Are you sure you're not going bald?" Ganya was teasing Sopan who self-consciously ran his fingers through his hair. "I think there is just a teeny-tiny bit of skin showing. It wasn't there yesterday. I bet your father went bald very early!"

"How do you know?" Sopan's eyes flashed.

"Have you ever seen him with hair? Maybe he never had any!" Ganya snickered, but took a step back, out of reach of Sopan's muscular arms. Now that Sarjya couldn't gambol around, Ganya helped out with the cows and even in the field when Prajakta couldn't; as a result, he seemed to be at their house all the time.

Sarjya sat up straighter, trying not to laugh. "*Arre* Ganya, stop with your strange theories. Let's ask my mother. Aai?"

"*Kay re*? What is it? Speak quickly, the tawa is getting hot!" Aai stepped out of the kitchen.

"Did Hanu Kaka ever have hair?"

"What? Good grief!" She slapped her forehead, leaving a white trail of flour. "You called me here to ask that? Of course, he had hair! In fact, it was dark and long, right until-" her words came to a choked stop with a quick glance at Sopan. "You kids really have nothing to do!" she muttered and hurried back to the fireplace.

An awkward silence followed. Ganya felt horrible for reminding his friend of his mother's death. Desperate to lighten the situation, Sarjya blurted out, "Now that we know Sopan will not go bald for some time yet, let's focus on names for Shaku's baby. I vote we call it Tanaji, if it's a boy!"

"No, no, there can never be another Tanaji!" Prajakta said, setting down the bunch of onions and chillies. "Besides, Shaku is certain she's having a girl!"

***

Swish, slash!

"Aah!" Sarjya winced as he put an end to his imaginary sword fight with the Mughals. He had thought swinging his arms around would be all right, but as his sister kept reminding him, *all the bones are connected, you silly boy!* He dragged himself to the door and looked around the courtyard for ways to amuse himself, but there wasn't a soul around.

The bored boy looked around for Kaloo, but even his faithful shadow had found more interesting things to do that day. *Sigh!* Sarjya leaned back against the wall. Only a few days more, then Baba had promised to let him walk with a stick. 'Your bone is healing well,' he had said and beamed, 'we can let you put a little pressure on it next week. But be extra careful, you've become plump with all the extra sweets your mother keeps feeding you for strength!'

Sarjya pulled his kurta away from his belly and grinned. That was certainly true – no activity and lots of milk, fruits and laddoos; not to mention food sent over by his adoring neighbours, had made him a podgy boy. He pinched his own cheeks; even that evil scar-faced Mughal couldn't carry him off now!

"What are you smiling about, and why are you halfway out of the house?" Aai tugged at his hand and said, "Come back inside!"

"Let me stay here *na*, Aai, I'm bored! At least I can watch people coming and going."

"Woof!"

Sarjya giggled as the dog slobbered all over his face. "You're not a puppy anymore. Ow, don't jump on my leg!"

"Prajakta, there you are!" Aai's voice became unusually loud. She watched her daughter check Sarjya's bandages and said, "My sister Shevanta has sent a message with a passing merchant, asking if you'll go to her in Sangamner to help out for a few months. She has injured her back, and I was thinking… anyway, Shaku is going, and her husband is sure to arrange a comfortable journey for her… You can go with her only. This way, she'll have company, and we can help Shevanta too. She raised me after our mother passed away when I was just a baby; I always feel indebted to her. Finally, I can be of some use to my sister!"

Sarjya watched Prajakta's face closely as their mother spoke; she gasped, then she beamed before saying, "Sure, Aai, it's our duty to help her now! But will you be able to manage without me now that Sarjya is laid up?"

Aai shrugged. "One day soon, you'll get married and go to your home, and then also we'll have to do without you, *na ga*?"

"In that case, I'll go. I'll miss you all so much in Sangamner, but, as you said, family is important!" Prajakta hugged her mother.

Sarjya stared at his sister – something was fishy here – the sheer joy radiating from her made him doubt her motives. Was this what she and Shaku had been whispering about? Curse this injury, his spy skills had been seriously impaired too!

For the next few days, Prajakta flitted about, humming and smiling to herself. Sarjya experienced a curious burning in his chest at the sight; he couldn't recollect a time in his life when they hadn't been together, except for those horrible days when that Mughal villain had stowed him in that miserable house near Kondana Fort. *Look at her – so happy and cheerful!* He scowled. *What about me lying here all injured and helpless? She doesn't care about me at all!*

"Why the sulky face?" Prajakta set aside the garlic she was peeling and squatted next to her little brother. "You're really this angry because I'm going with Shaku? It's only for a few months; besides, what will you do there? I'll have to do all girly jobs there, and you'd hate to help with those! Also, Aai and Baba need you here, especially now that you can move around a bit." She ruffled his hair and said, "Baba's treatment and Aai's *haldi doodh* and prayers have got you standing up superfast!"

Sarjya kept his eyes screwed shut. He heard her sigh and then walk off, taking the scent of garlic with her. When he finally opened his eyes, the tears he was holding in overflowed onto his cheeks. Everything Prajakta said was true; he had Kaloo, Ganya, Sopan and his parents here, so why did he feel this inexplicable despair? Should he have rested for some more time? But that would have meant remaining in bed, and he was itching to get out of the house. Sarjya hobbled to the courtyard; maybe the happenings in Naikwadi could provide a distraction from his grief.

"That nearly fell, be careful!" Shaku's husband was supervising the two men carrying a huge wooden trunk. "Oh, hello Sarjya! Good to see you on your feet again!" He saw the curiosity on the boy's face and said,

"That's for packing all the stuff Shaku's carrying back to Sangamner. *Arre, arre,* you're going to drop it!" He hurried after the men.

Sarjya sighed. Another reminder of his sister going away! Prajakta had Shaku, her best friend – why would she want to be with her baby brother? What on earth could he do except look on helplessly?

He watched the party make its way to the end of the village with narrowed eyes. The men tottered down the sunlit path with the gigantic trunk. Why was Shaku taking so much luggage? That box was almost large enough to fit… hmmm… Sarjya's lips stretched into a wide smile. Enough of lying indoors and brooding, it was time for another adventure!

Chapter 3

"Don't cry, Aai, you only told me to go to Sangamner! Do you want me to stay here?" Prajakta smiled at her bawling mother, who maintained a death grip on the bullock cart. They held hands, watching while the two men who worked for Shaku's husband loaded the cart. The first item to go aboard was the enormous ornate wooden trunk, which took up half the space in the cart; it was full of presents for Shaku's parents. Shaku's husband had insisted on sending a whole load of spices, wool, clothes, and even a carpet! Prajakta shivered and looked past Aai to the foggy outlines of the houses in the village. "Where did Sarjya go?"

Aai turned back with a frown. "He was just here with Ganya. God knows where they both went!"

"Sopan, have you seen Sarjya?"

Sopan blew on his palms and clapped them together. "Brrr! No Kaku." He grinned at Prajakta and said, "Try not to return with new pets as a replacement for your *ghorpad*!" He was referring to the monitor lizard that had followed Prajakta home one day from the forest, and then played a pivotal role in the Battle for Kondana.

"Hmmm," Prajakta said, eyes still searching for her brother. *Where on earth has he disappeared to? Isn't he going to see me off? After all, Sangamner is a long way off, and it might be months before we meet again.*

"What is it, Tai?" Sopan asked.

"Sarjya," Prajakta said, looking at Sopan. She rubbed her forehead and tried not to cry. "He didn't say goodbye. Perhaps he's really angry that I'm going, maybe I shouldn't..."

"*Aga* Tai, don't worry. You know how our Sarjya is, his anger rises like the milk boiling over, and settles down just as fast! Ganya and I will be with him, don't think so much!"

The oxen moved restlessly, and the sound of their bells echoed through the silence. Baba came over to Prajakta and patted her on her head. "Take care, child! May Lord Mahadev be with you and protect you both!"

The cart driver clicked his tongue, and the wooden structure jerked as the oxen got ready to depart. Shaku and Prajakta climbed onto one side, the other being laden with their luggage. Aai wiped her eyes with her *padar* and sniffed. Prajakta gave her a tremulous smile and waved goodbye. *Is it evil of me to be relieved to get away from Naikwadi for a while? Should I never have hatched this plan?* Her stomach burned with questions as the sight of her parents, Shaku's husband and Sopan grew fainter. Was that Sarjya she saw joining them? Prajakta waved furiously, hoping her brother wouldn't stay mad at her for long. "Goodbye, I'll miss you!" she shouted to him.

Three hours later, the cart halted for a break and water.

"Are you alright?" Shaku whispered as Prajakta helped her climb up again.

Prajakta looked at her friend with suspiciously bright eyes. "What? I'm perfectly okay!" She kicked the wooden trunk in frustration and winced at the jarring pain in her foot. "What could possibly be wrong?" she mumbled as the oxen picked up a gentle pace.

Shaku wished *Aho* hadn't told the cart driver to take extra care and drive slowly; at this rate, she would have the child, and he would be old enough to marry before they reached Sangamner! There were two men with the cart, so they could take turns driving through the night. She looked at the sheer amount of luggage – maybe she shouldn't have brought so many things! But *Aho* had been firm, insisting, "I want you to be comfortable there when winter comes, and to enjoy the break from household work. Besides, my in-laws should also know their daughter is now accustomed to luxury. Just make sure you have a girl!" he had whispered to her.

Shaku rubbed her back and tried not to groan aloud. If there was less stuff, the oxen could have run so much faster! Did the baby really need two dozen clothes? Overcome with frustration, Shaku glared at the elaborately carved box; then she blinked. Was it not fastened properly? *Arre Deva!* Now, the fog would enter and ruin all her precious things! She nudged Prajakta, who was still staring back at the path they had left behind. "Help me up, the trunk is not shut properly. All the things inside will get damp."

The girls stood up slowly, holding onto each other in the gently rocking cart. They tried to push down the lid together.

"Aaah!" Prajakta screamed.

The cart driver pulled the reins, and the oxen came to a halt. Shaku stumbled and grabbed onto her friend to prevent falling out of the cart. "What on earth?" She gaped at Prajakta.

"Something is moving inside!" Prajakta said, her dark eyes staring out from a suddenly bloodless face.

"What rubbish!" Shaku clutched her friend. "Really?"

"*Kay jhala muli*?" The two men ran to the back of the cart and asked.

"Kaka, there's an animal inside this box!"

"Step back, girls!" The man urged the girls to get off. Then they raised their sturdy sticks and lifted the lid in unison. Joint exclamations of surprise escaped them, and they suddenly lowered their sticks.

"What? What is it?" The girls couldn't see past the tall men. "Is it a wolf or a panther?"

The men's shoulders shook with laughter as they bent down to pull out a cowering nine-year-old boy.

"Sarjya?" Prajakta clapped her hand to her forehead. "How in the blazes did you get in there? Did you get locked inside by mistake?" Prajakta shook her brother vigorously, ignoring his protests. Shaku lowered herself to the ground, too shaken for words.

"Tai! Tai, stop shaking me!" Sarjya squealed. He looked up at her and swallowed. "I…I did this intentionally." His lips quivered in half a smile at the way his sister's jaw dropped open, then he composed his face. "Sorry! I didn't want to stay apart from you for so many months!" His words tumbled over each other. He looked at his elder sister, fury radiating from her face, and pleaded, "Tai, say something." He had really messed up this time. Sarjya limped to one side of the cart where Shaku was gasping for breath on the ground next to the wheel. *I'm such an idiot!* He cursed himself. When would he learn not to act on the very first impulse that ran through his mind? He dropped his face onto his palms and began to sob.

"Hush, it's okay," the whisper made Sarjya raise his head to find his sister at his side. She squatted next to him and put her arm around his shoulders. "It'll be all right, Sarjya, don't cry!"

"So, what are we going to do now?" The cart driver, hands on his waist, asked, "Go back and deposit this rascal, or keep going onward?"

Prajakta turned to Shaku, who nodded, then she smiled at the hope in her brother's eyes. "Let's keep going, Kaka, but we'll stop at the next village and send word to our Baba."

Sarjya felt a twinge of guilt at her words, but it was quickly washed away by the surge of delight that washed over him at being allowed to stay with her; he beamed and leapt up to hug his sister who squealed, "Enough, enough, let go of me, I can't breathe! At least you haven't brought your comrade in mischief along with you!" She laughed, then paled at the expression on his face. "You didn't!"

"No, no Tai, but-" Sarjya let out in a low voice.

Shaku and Prajakta both groaned at his words.

"Ganya wouldn't fit in the trunk with me! But I had to get Kaloo along."

As if on cue, a torrent of barks emerged from the trunk. Prajakta leapt up into the cart and scooped up the dog, who licked her face in glee. "Kaloo, what to do with your master?" Then she slapped her forehead and shrugged. "What's done is done, let's think how you can be of use to Shevanta Mavshi in Sangamner now."

"I hope you both haven't damaged any of my things," Shaku grumbled, grinning to show she wasn't really angry. The bells on the oxen jingled merrily as they made their way in the rosy glow of the setting sun. As the travellers passed near a fort, Sarjya stood up for a better view. "Kaka, is that Salher Fort?"

The man chuckled. "No, no, boy! Salher is much further away, near Nashik."

"I've heard so much about it!" Sarjya's eyes lit up as he spoke, "Parshuram flung his axe, and it landed there. And there's a temple on top of the fort with huge footprints in the rock, nearly four times the size of human feet! And, didn't a battle take place there recently? I heard Shivaji Raje's men totally routed the Mughals!"

"Yes, boy," the cart driver said with pride, "Salher and Mulher were both captured by us. One of my cousins fought with Prataprao Gujar and Moropant Pingale in that battle. Our entire village celebrated for three days!"

The other man snorted, "And that Aurangzeb went mad with rage! He recalled Jaswant Singh and the Rajput commander from Aurangabad, and now plans to send someone else to wreak havoc there."

"Why is Salher so important for us?" Prajakta asked.

"It's of immense strategic importance. Salher is the highest fort in the Sahyadris, and a great vantage point to oversee all the important trade routes and thereby control them."

Prajakta shuddered. "Every man our soldiers kill, that madman Aurangzeb replaces with an even more violent one. They just keep coming!"

As if on cue, a loud howl arose from the nearby trees, making all three children and the dog squeal and cling to each other. The men lifted their lanterns and made loud noises to scare away potential predators. The nervous oxen moved faster, their jingling bells the only sound in the growing darkness. When no more noises arose from around them for a long time, everyone breathed sighs of relief.

It was morning when the cart finally halted again. Sarjya rubbed his eyes and tottered to his feet. He looked around interestedly, then jumped off the cart onto the grass underneath. "Brrr, it's cold!" he said, rubbing his arms.

Prajakta was the next to wake up; she nudged Shaku and helped her out. The fog was lifting, and shafts of the morning sun were beginning to break through. The few villagers out for morning ablutions gave them curious looks, and a couple of stray dogs ran up to sniff the newcomers, making the oxen bellow nervously. Kaloo raised his head; the scent of his fellow canines must have reached his nose, for he shook himself and leapt off the cart to join his master.

"Ewww!" Sarjya shouted, scrunching his nose, "You jumped right into the cow dung, Kaloo! Stop, you idiot, don't rub against my legs!"

A middle-aged woman in a dark green saree was walking rapidly towards them, followed by a limping man. "You reached already!" She beamed at Shaku and enveloped her in a hug. "My, you are glowing, *pori*! We missed you every day." Prajakta watched as joyful tears rained down her face. The man now caught up with them, and he rested his hand on Shaku's head.

"Baba!" she cried and clung to him.

Prajakta and Sarjya looked at each other nervously. Where was Shevanta Mavshi?

Shaku's mom wiped her eyes and turned to the brother-sister duo. She blinked at Sarjya, then smiled. "Welcome, children! Shevanta Tai told me to greet you and bring you home. Her back hurts terribly, and she's unable to get out of bed; it'll be such a blessing to have you around for help. I heard your father is a healer. Has he sent anything for her pain?" She turned to look at the small cloud of dust moving towards them. "Here come the boys!"

Sarjya blinked rapidly as two mini tornadoes screeched to a halt beside them.

"Hello!" Both spoke in unison.

"I'm Pandurang."

"And I'm Vitthal!"

They beamed. "You're a boy! We thought only a girl was coming. We've come to help with the luggage."

Shaku's mother put her arm around Prajakta's shoulders. "These monkeys are Shaku's nephews, they are twins," she added unnecessarily, for anyone looking at the two grinning faces would have guessed that in an instant.

"*Husha,* now I won't have to spend the next few weeks with only girls for company!" Sarjya blurted out.

Loud laughter rang out, and the morning sun suddenly felt warmer. The two drivers carried the bulk of the luggage, and the trio of boys and Prajakta quickly moved the rest. Shaku and her parents brought up the rear, the two women chatting all the way, while Shaku's father just beamed with joy; his daughter was back! As the noisy group walked home, the villagers came to their doors to greet them. The group came to a halt outside a small house where many women were bustling in and out of the open door.

"Here's Shevanta Tai's house," Shaku's mother smiled and said. "The village women are taking turns to help her out with the chores and cooking. She'll be so happy that you've come, Prajakta!"

It took only a couple of days for Prajakta and Sarjya to adjust to their new routine at Sangamner. Sarjya helped in the fields and played with the boys, and Prajakta cooked, cleaned and looked after their aunt. She tried to emulate the village women – they did everything so effortlessly – one hand would swing down to pick up the kneaded dough and then quickly pat out a *bhakri,* while the other could stir the lentils or peel the onions, or even soothe a crying baby. Prajakta marvelled at their multitasking skills – the only time she felt confident was when someone was injured or in pain. Baba's lessons on herbs and decoctions would flash through her mind, and she'd hurry to make a poultice or clean the wound. As their aunt slowly sat up and then gradually walked, word of Prajakta's healing skills spread, and the villagers of Sangamner began to consult her for their aches and pains, especially now that winter was setting in. The children missed their home, but they were busy most of the time, and Kaloo's licks and cuddles helped ease the novelty of being outsiders.

But the idyll was short-lived, and a few weeks later, the rumours began to reach even their quiet little place.

'Aurangzeb is sending a huge army!'

'My cousin saw a large cloud of dust – there were thousands of men on horses!' one boy muttered.

'The Mughal is crazy with anger and desperate to wipe out the Marathas!' a villager repeated a rumour.

Prajakta grew paler with every new piece of gossip, but Shevanta Mavshi remained unconcerned, "Shivaji Raje will not let anything happen to us!"

Chapter 4

Sangamner was much larger than Naikwadi, but it was still a closely knit community that wholeheartedly believed in the cause of Hindavi Swarajya. Many of the young men had sworn to support their King, and had been trained by his trusted soldiers. The villagers had fond memories of the time Raje had visited their village.

"Such a radiant face!" one of the women said with a sigh, as she pulled up her bucket from the well. "I would follow him anywhere." She turned to the woman, struggling with a fidgety baby at her waist and asked, "Haven't you named your son Shiva?"

The chubby boy stopped his escape venture and gurgled as the women cooed over him. "I hope he will grow up to be as majestic as our King!" His mother gave a shy smile.

Prajakta watched the ease with which the women interacted; they knew everything about each other's families.

"*Aga* Manda, how is your husband's foot now? *Deva Deva,* how swollen it was yesterday when the men helped him back from the fields!"

"Much better now!" The woman turned to Prajakta and said, "Your onion poultice worked wonders, and I'm giving him *haldi doodh* two times a day."

"I hope he's keeping the foot elevated," Prajakta said, moving forward hesitantly. The circle of women parted to let her in. Their warm smiles and approving looks helped her jaw unclench; they were just like her people at Naikwadi!

"Tai!"

Prajakta turned around at the shout, and felt the world spin for a brief instant at the sight before her. Just a minute ago, when she had told Sarjya she was going to get water from the well, his kurta had been a pristine white. Now the crying boy's clothes were a blotchy red mess. Sarjya clutched his left hand in agony and mutely looked to his big sister for help. Gulping, she willed the darkness before her eyes to recede; then she dropped the brass pot and sprinted towards her brother. "What happened?" she asked, putting an arm around Sarjya and helping him sit on the ground.

"Tai, Tai," he sobbed, his breath hitching as he desperately tried to breathe.

"Shh, shh. Shh," she patted his back and whispered, "Close your eyes and take a deep breath. Now, tell me what happened."

Sarjya looked into his sister's worried eyes and gave a tiny sob; then he blew out his breath before he spoke, "I was only… I…" his shoulders slumped, "I guess I did it again… behaved foolishly!" Looking at his woebegone expression, Prajakta felt the beginnings of a smile. Then, worry overpowered everything else, and she urged him to tell her what had transpired.

Sarjya drew a shuddering breath, then drew strength from her steely gaze. "Pandurang, Vitthal, and I were playing near the village walls." Prajakta's expression made him swallow, before he rushed to add, "We were staying within the boundaries of the village only! Pandurang is great at sculpting – he made a *shivling* with wet mud, and we put a few *bel patras* on it with some flowers, and we prayed to Lord Mahadev." He was quiet for a while as he figured out how to best frame the next few words. "Then I got… um… inspired by Shivaji Raje and said we should also take the oath of Swarajya."

Prajakta hissed, already beginning to dread what was coming next. Everyone in the land knew how Shivaji Raje, as a young boy, had taken the oath of Swaraj in the Sri Raireshwar temple along with his Mavalas by cutting his little finger and offering a blood sacrifice to Lord Mahadev. Prajakta shook her head at her little brother, clutching his left hand as she realized he had tried to emulate his hero. "Aai Bhavani!" she prayed, hoping the cut was only a superficial one. She unwrapped the grimy cloth pressed against it. A wave of nausea threatened to overwhelm her – the tip of the little finger was nearly separate from the rest of his hand – it only hung by a minuscule strip of skin. Prajakta pressed the cloth back onto the wound, wincing at the yelp that Sarjya gave. She thought furiously – what would Baba do? For a while, no ideas came to mind. Then, the mist lifted, and she heard her father's strong voice speak in a low, calm register. *First, wash the wound and make sure no dirt, grass or leaves are sticking to it. Sometimes you may even find rust particles.*

Prajakta ran back to the well to get some water in her pot, then squatted next to her brother, slowly pouring it over his wound. Sarjya howled in pain, then noticed the gawking women and tried to damp down the sounds involuntarily escaping him.

"*Aga bai, kay jhala?*"

"*Deva, Deva,* so much blood!"

Their high-pitched comments escalated, and Prajakta fought the urge to shush the ladies; instead she focussed on cleaning the wound. Would she be able to reattach the finger? She had never seen Baba do such a thing, though he had stitched up Kanta Kaku's arm when his sickle had sliced it. Could she do that here? But the piece with the tip of the finger didn't look large enough to allow any needle to go through it.

And it was already turning black. What should she do? Prajakta thought frantically for a few seconds, then decided to just bandage the finger and hope for the best.

She mopped the wound and pressed tightly till the bleeding slowed, then splinted the rest of the little finger to the ring finger for support. Now clean and dry, Sarjya's hand looked infinitely better. The boy wiped his tears and said, "Tai, you're just as good as Baba, thank you!"

Prajakta smiled at her brother. "It'll all be better soon, don't worry! You wait here, I'll go and get some more water."

The women at the well moved aside for her to draw the water first, then as the brother-sister duo slowly walked back to their aunt's house, the gossip resumed behind them.

"What will you tell Aai and Baba?" Sarjya asked.

Prajakta hefted the pot higher at her waist, causing a little water to slosh onto her bloodied *parkar*. "We'll cross that bridge when we come to it. Right now, let's concentrate on your healing. Once Shaku's baby is born, both of us should return home."

"We will?" Sarjya brightened. "I miss Aai-Baba… and Ganya and Sopan too. I even miss Maloji Kaka, the surly headman! Everyone here is very friendly, but-" he stopped.

"Yes," Prajakta sighed, "but it's not home." She ruffled her little brother's hair with her free hand.

Vitthal and Pandurang ran up to them. "Sarjya, are you alright?"

Sarjya was uncharacteristically silent.

"What is it, *Bhau*? Are you angry at us? We got so scared when the bleeding started; we thought you were going to die!" Vitthal said.

"And our mother would thrash us for being a part of it!" Pandurang added, "So we ran away, but then we realized we should have been there for our friend." He looked down at Sarjya's bandaged hand.

"And so, we returned to our *shivling*, but you were gone!" Vitthal moved his hands around as if to demonstrate how Sarjya had vanished into thin air. "Only blood remained near the flowers!" He gave a sheepish smile and said, "We thought… we were sure you became a sacrifice to Mahadev!"

"We both cried our hearts out!" Pandurang jumped in to add, "then prayed to God for your soul!"

"Stop it, you two!" Sarjya wasn't sure whether to yell at them or laugh. "Your imagination is too wild! I would have appreciated some help, though."

"Sorry!" the boys chorused, "we won't do it again!"

Prajakta bristled. "No one is doing any of that again. *Chal* Sarjya!" The indignant girl began walking, her brother trailing after her. They were closely followed by Pandurang and Vitthal with despondent faces.

'Will you tell our mother?'

'Will you never talk to us again?'

Their plaintive questions followed Prajakta and Sarjya all the way back to the village.

Sarjya's finger stopped hurting in a few days, but the nearly cut-off end began to shrivel up and dry. "The blood supply is not reaching the tip," Prajakta explained to the worried boy as she dressed the wound, trying to ignore the twins peeping over her shoulders with curiosity.

"You'll have 4 ½ fingers now!" Vitthal whispered.

"Total 9 ½!" Pandurang added.

"You…!" Prajakta's face darkened. She pressed her fists to her sides to stop herself from boxing their ears. "By the way," she said, "where did you get the sword from that day?"

"I… we…," Pandurang stammered.

"We… I…," Vitthal whispered.

"They stole it from their neighbour's house!" Sarjya was delighted to watch them turn red.

Prajakta's eyes narrowed. "Is that so?" She inhaled sharply, then said, "I think you should try to be better friends from now on. Did Shivaji Raje's Mavalas turn tail and run off if he was ever in trouble? Weren't you all trying to emulate our King?"

"Yes, Tai!" the twins echoed.

Their morose expression made Sarjya's heart melt. "*Chal jau de,* let's go and look for that nest that we found that day. Do you think eggs will have hatched?"

"No climbing trees!" Prajakta yelled after the running boys.

"Yes!" The wind carried their words and giggles back to her.

Aai Bhavani, what will these boys do next? She shook her head ruefully. *I should get to work on replenishing my stock of marigold ointment; there are still some flowers left in the fields.* Prajakta headed to the fields and returned home with a handful of flowers, stems and leaves. *What proportion of beeswax and oil had Baba used?* She imagined the potentially disastrous situations Sarjya could get into if asked to look for honeycombs, and decided to request one of the village men for help. The combination of mischievous boys and angry bees was just too much for her to deal with this week!

"Take care, *my boy*!" The old woman wiped her tears with her padar.

"Aai, don't cry! You know how easily we won last time, *na*? Nothing will happen to me." The young man hugged his mother.

Prajakta glanced down at his bundle of belongings and the spear on the ground. *Would this war never end?* She stole another look at the man – the wispy moustache gave away his tender age – only a boy still! As Prajakta hurried home, she saw another woman, her eyes moist, performing *aarti* and bidding her husband goodbye. *So many men are going off to battle, something big is happening!* But they hadn't heard of any threat, especially after Salher had been captured. *So where were all these men headed?*

"I told you not to go out!" Radha Mavshi was scolding Shaku gently, "It's getting chilly in the field, especially in the morning. If you catch a cold, the baby will get one too!"

"Mavshi?" One of the villagers stood at the door.

Radha Mavshi rushed out. "*Kay re*?"

"Shaku's husband has sent a message."

"Yes, yes!" She beamed. "When is he reaching here? Hopefully, before the child is born!"

"Actually," the man's face fell as he added, "he has sent word that a large army is approaching Nashik, and another one led by Diler Khan was heading towards Pune. He can't reach here, and has insisted everyone stay put and not go anywhere near Pune."

Prajakta and Sarjya gasped, "But what about our village? Aai and Baba?"

Refusing to meet their eyes, the man muttered, "I…I don't know… I just know what I was told."

"Naikwadi is a little further away from Pune," Radha Mavshi rushed to say, "I'm sure they're all fine, children."

Prajakta's heart sputtered and stopped.

"Child, are you alright? You've gone white!" She rushed to help the girl to the ground. "Sarjya, go get your sister some water!"

Prajakta sipped the water, but the fluid refused to go down; Radha Mavshi had to thump her back and urge her to look up. Prajakta winced; once the constriction eased, she took a few more sips of water before glancing at her brother. It was beginning to dawn on him too that their parents and their village were in grave danger. The two hugged each other, refusing to voice the awful thoughts that raced through their minds.

Later that night, when everyone was asleep, Sarjya scooched closer to his sister. "Tai, can we borrow a horse and ride back home? Tai, are you sleeping?"

"No, I'm thinking." Prajakta was surprised she was seriously considering Sarjya's suggestion. Most of his ideas were ill-thought-out and ended in disaster, but how could they sleep peacefully until they knew their parents were safe?

Chapter 5

A few weeks later, children woke up to utter silence. They stepped out into the alley and looked around the courtyard; they had never experienced such an absence of sound – even the stray dogs and chickens were quiet. Sarjya shook his head, then tilted it from side to side.

"What are you doing?"

"No sound. Like a fog inside my head. Sometimes this happens when water goes in my ears, so I was just checking if that's the case now!"

Prajakta cuffed him. "Something has happened! Everyone is moving towards the headman's house." She dodged the two men walking past and muttering, '*Nirdayi, papi!*' Prajakta rubbed her arms as a sudden icy sensation moved over her, as if she had walked into a haunted house. "*Om Namah Shivaya, Om Namah Shivay!*" she whispered.

"Tai!" Sarjya shook her elbow and said, "What is it? Why are you praying?"

Prajakta mutely dragged her brother to the headman's house, where a large crowd had gathered. Santaji, the village headman, stood tall above the now audible murmuring of his people. Prajakta thought of Maloji Kaka, the thin, serious headman of Naikwadi village, and suddenly longed for her own people. She pulled her trembling brother closer, damping down the desperate need to sprout wings and fly home. Santaji raised his palm for silence. "My brothers and sisters," he faltered, "we… I have received news," the man swallowed once, then continued, "Diler Khan has attacked Pune!"

A collective gasp arose from the men and women. Sarjya whimpered and grasped Prajakta's hand for support.

The headman continued to be the bearer of more bad news. "His men killed mercilessly; they mowed down everyone in sight … even women and older children. Pune now lies in shambles… a smouldering pile of blood and ashes!" His breath hitched, "and…"

There was more? Some women began to wail. *My son… my father…* anguish arose from the people. Sarjya looked at his sister and whispered, "Tai?"

She put her fingers over her lips and shook her head. "No, no, they must be fine."

"And," Santaji continued, "the other news that has reached us is that the Mughals have laid siege to Salher!"

"How is that possible?" a young man shouted. "We just got control of the fort!"

The headman sighed. "Bahadur Khan left Surat and moved towards Supa, and Diler Khan entered Pune around the same time. The supply lines are now threatened…"

"But Pune, what happened there?" A grey-haired man tottered forward. "How many …who… how will we know if our loved ones are safe?"

The solemn look on Santaji's face spoke volumes. No one was safe. Prajakta felt as if a giant had grabbed her throat and was slowly choking the life out of her.

"My Aai and Baba!" Sarjya spoke up. All eyes turned to the boy. "They are in Naikwadi. Does anyone know if my village was affected?"

The headman hung his head. "Child, I only know no adult in Pune was spared."

A wail broke out from the woman next to Prajakta. She grabbed her brother's hand and quickly exited the place.

"But… wait, Tai! We don't… we need to find out…."

"No one has more news, Sarjya," Prajakta snapped. "That's all they know; everyone was killed. Only the very small children were spared."

Sarjya's jaw dropped. "Sopan and Ganya…?

"Could be." Prajakta's shoulders shook. "We just need to pray now… that Naikwadi was not on the Mughal route, that it was too insignificant for them."

Prajakta was restless for the next two weeks. Shaku tried to console her friend, but she was with her family, and her own husband was safely in Bijapur. *Why had she made that silly plan to come here? What was the point of living if…* Prajakta's thoughts did not let her days go by without anguish, and the darkness came with its own nightmares. The brother-sister duo hung around the village gates all day, asking any visitor for news.

"Prajakta!" It was Shaku with some bhakris and onions for her and Sarjya. "Eat something. How thin you both have become in such a short time!"

"I'm not hungry," they chorused.

Shaku smiled. "You are beginning to sound like Pandurang and Vitthal!" She turned to Sarjya and said, "I thought you always stayed positive. Isn't Shivaji Raje your hero?"

"Yes!" His eyes flashed once, then resumed their dull look.

"Then behave like him! Did he feel scared when the huge Afzal Khan approached him?"

"Of course not!"

"Did Raje accept he would be a prisoner of that despot Aurangzeb and resign himself to his fate?"

Sarjya shook his head.

Shaku smiled at the boy and said, "Then why should you fear anything? All will turn out fine. Aai Bhavani will protect us all!"

As if in benediction, the rays of the rising sun bathed the spot where they were standing, and dispelled the fog. The trio stood there, shoulder to shoulder, watching the able-bodied young men leave the village one by one.

"Where are they headed, Tai?" Sarjya asked.

One of the men heard him and put down his bundle of belongings. His huge moustache bristled as he spoke, "We are heading for Salher. We cannot let it fall to the Mughals. Diler Khan is marching to join Bahadur Khan with 30,000 more men; we need to bolster the strength of our own army."

"How many men does Bahadur Khan already have there?" Sarjya asked.

"Fifty thousand!"

The children gasped and fell silent.

"Don't worry." The young soldier lifted his belongings and flexed his biceps. "See these muscles? Each Maratha is equivalent to 10 Mughals! We will send them packing in no time!"

January, 1672

"Tai, have you heard about the siege of Panhala Fort?"

"The one in which Raje was trapped for many months, and they say the Siddi did not allow even an ant to get outside?"

Sarjya nodded. "Vitthal and Pandurang were talking about it, and it got me thinking… what if Salher is also like that? What if our men need help? They are totally surrounded!"

"Don't underestimate Shivaji Raje and his men. His plans always succeed; he is always three steps ahead of his enemies at all times. Didn't you listen to that gondhali singer last week at the prayer meeting the headman held? He sang about how the mighty Baji Prabhu, with only three hundred men, held off over three thousand of Adil Shah's men till Raje reached Vishalgad. How intricate their plans were – so many little things came together to combine into one brilliant strategy! Salher is too important to lose; we've held it for a year now."

"Sarjya!" Vitthal and Pandurang were jumping up and down like monkeys. Prajakta looked at their beaming faces and felt her spirits lift. "What is it? Has any news come for us?"

"Yes. Shaku's baby is coming!"

"Oh!" Prajakta had hoped for news of Aai and Baba, but this was good news too; once the baby was born, she would ask her Mavshi to help her and Sarjya go back to Naikwadi. They felt trapped here in Sangamner, despite all the love they had received. She rushed to Shaku's house with the boys close at her heels.

Sarjya and the twins got bored after an hour. "Still no baby?" they asked.

"Asking every time she screams will not hasten the process!" Prajakta fanned herself; despite the cold, it was stifling inside. The obvious pain her friend was in scared her – for Shaku and for her own possible future, but she didn't let that show on her face. Over the next interminably slow hours, Sarjya's words kept resonating through Prajakta's mind. Was there anything they could do to help the cause of Swarajya from here? She wished they were in Naikwadi again, where gunpowder, cannonballs, and so much more were being produced for the war effort. Salher was more than 80 kos from Sangamner; the area was not well-suited to the usual guerrilla warfare in which the Mavalas had been so successful. Defeating Aurangzeb's army on open land was unheard of. She shook her head free of all the conflicting thoughts and gripped her best friend's hand tightly. "Breathe," she told Shaku as her mother urged her to sip some water.

When the shrill cry of the newborn roused the sleeping boys, they jumped to their feet and ran in only to collide with Prajakta.

"Oh, my head!"

"My hand!"

"Woof, woof!" Kaloo jumped around the children, nearly tripping them up.

Prajakta rubbed her shoulder where Vitthal had run smack into her, then moved Sarjya into the light of the lantern. "Is your hand ok? The wound is not bleeding, *na*?"

He rubbed his hair vigorously, making it stand up like a porcupine; then he blinked in the flickering light. "I'm fine, Tai. Is it a girl or a boy?"

"It's a girl! Shaku's mother came out of the house with a mewling bundle in her arms. "Lakshmi has arrived!" She bent to allow the boys a look.

"Why is she so red?" Vitthal asked.

"Oh, she is so ugly, like Kaloo!" Pandurang said.

Prajakta cuffed the two boys and looked at Shaku's mom with concern, but she didn't appear to be offended.

"What do you boys know?" she said, laughing, "All babies look the same at first. *Chal* Prajakta, help me get some more hot water, and you monkeys go to sleep now."

The trio walked back to the courtyard where they were sleeping on piles of hay.

"*Kay re*, you called my Kaloo ugly?" Sarjya shoved Pandurang.

"Oh, sorry! He's so handsome, we should make him our King!" the boy teased.

"Yes, he should be King of all the dogs!" Sarjya bristled. "He's extremely intelligent!" As if sensing his words, the dog snuggled closer to his beloved master and gave a short bark. The children laughed and lay down too.

Shaku's mother listened to the soft whimpers of her newborn granddaughter, the boys' laughter, and the low hums of Prajakta as she readied fresh clothes for her friend. "Thank you, Aai Bhavani, for this day. May our loved ones always remain healthy and happy!" she whispered.

"Kaku?"

Prajakta peeped from the doorway. It was a beggar. She looked at the bent-over, haggard old fellow and felt sad for him.

"Who is it?" Shevanta Mavshi walked out for a look. "Prajakta, get some water and those guavas Sarjya plucked yesterday."

"May Aai Bhavani bless you!" The man suddenly stood straighter and smiled.

"*Arre Deva,* it's you, Surya! Your disguises are always perfect!" Shevanta Mavshi beamed.

Prajakta's jaw dropped. It was a young man! He gave her a mischievous glance, then took a bite of the guava she brought.

"Any news from Pune, Surya? My sister and her husband are there."

Prajakta inhaled sharply. *This must be one of Shivaji's spies who travelled all over the land in disguise and reported back to him.*

The young man chewed slowly, then shook his head. "The scoundrels razed everything to the ground – no man or woman left alive."

"My family is at Naikwadi, near Pune. Was that… did they….?" Shevanta faltered, her hand gripping her niece's shoulder.

Surya's face brightened just a little. "No, the surrounding villages were not touched; the Mughals just seemed hellbent on destroying Pune and everything it represented." His fake white moustache quivered.

"Thank God!" Shevanta sank to her feet. "We were all so worried." She turned to Prajakta and said, "Run inside, child, and get the laadoos we made. Surya," she beamed at the man, "you must take them with you. First, for the great joy you brought us by telling us this, and also because my back is totally fine now!"

"Thank you, Kaku," Surya said as he put the sweets in his cloth bag. "I will be leaving tonight for Salher with some messages. We may not meet..." his voice grew rough, "... for some time. Take care."

"You too, my child." Shevanta placed her right palm on his head and murmured, "my blessings and prayers are with you. Aai Bhavani will protect you from all harm."

Later that evening, they also learned that Diler Khan had definitely moved out with the bulk of his army towards Salher after levelling Pune, and that Shivaji Raje was making arrangements to send wagons filled with grain to help the people living in the affected areas.

"Can we go home now, Tai?" Sarjya tugged at her skirt. "Or will Diler Khan be on the road we need to take?"

"No child," their uncle spoke, "the Mughal army has already reached Nashik."

"So, we can go home, Kaka?" Prajakta's hopeful gaze and Sarjya's wistful face made the man smile.

"I will see what can be done to send you as soon as we can."

Sarjya and Prajakta beamed at each other. Aai and Baba were safe, and they were finally going home!

Chapter 6

April, 1674
Raigad

The man stood poised at the edge of the cliff. He kicked a pebble and watched as it rolled and gained speed to vanish into the darkness a long, long way below. Overhead, the clouds moved to swiftly engulf the moon, calling down a sheet of darkness so dense he couldn't see his pale hands in front of his face. He loved to come here late at night when all the inhabitants of the fort were in bed. Sleep had eluded him for months now – two years and two months to be precise – ever since they brought him news of that tragedy. He'd work throughout the day, losing himself in his craft and taking on more work than anyone could do; then the people around him would return to their families, and he'd trudge back to stare blankly at the walls, hoping he could lull his mind to sleep. After a few hours of tossing and turning, he'd walk out into the inky black night with only howling dogs and crickets for company. Looking at the stars sometimes brought him solace, but not today.

He had watched the colourfully dressed children and women in festive saris stand by their men and worship the *gudi,* and eat offerings of jaggery and neem leaves. For them, it was the start of a new year; for him, it was one more day of wishing he were dead. The sight of a chubby little boy tightly gripping his father's hand as he climbed up the temple steps had made him want to weep. Now, with no one around to pity him or try to console him with mundane words, he finally allowed himself to do that. Tears rolled down his gaunt face, then loud sobs racked his body, and he cried for the loss of his beautiful family.

A cough somewhere behind. He hurriedly wiped his face and whirled around. Couldn't he even grieve in peace?

"I'm sorry to intrude." The soft voice was almost inaudible. Then, the clouds parted to reveal the speaker in the moonlight. The gentle words didn't quite suit the bearded giant who stood before him. Fair, sharp-featured and piercing green eyes – danger radiated from every pore of the man.

He frowned – the face, the voice, the cadence – this man was not from around here! Instantly wary, he moved away from the edge of the cliff, all the while keeping one hand on the dagger at his waist.

"I know you are in pain." The words were spoken in Hindi this time, reminding him of his childhood home.

"Who are you?"

"Ahmed." The giant smiled.

"You're a long way from home! I should report you to the King's men. What do you want with me?"

"To share your sorrows, to sit a while with you in the darkness."

A bitter laugh escaped the man. "You look like a soldier and talk like a poet! Thank you, but I don't need your help." He turned and started walking away.

"I know you hate Shivaji!"

The man froze at the softly whispered words. How did he…? He looked around, but there was no one else to overhear his secret.

Clenching his fists, he turned and asked, "What do you want? Pearls? Gold? Name your price!"

Ahmed's laughter echoed through the night, making the man look around nervously and put a finger over his lips. "I'm not here to blackmail you. Besides, I know you have the skills to take whatever you need at any time."

"Then why are you here?"

"Believe it or not, I'm your well-wisher. I have lost a lot too due to that Shivaji!" Ahmed hissed. "I'm desperate for him to be brought to his knees, and I have the perfect plan for it!" Ahmed smiled at the flare of interest in the man's eyes.

The man led Ahmed over to an alcove in the ramparts, and peeped over the ledge and all around to make sure they were alone. "First, tell me who sent you?"

"I have like-minded friends in high places, but I have come here alone. We know you have sacrificed a lot for a cause you never even believed in, and that you are one of the few intelligent people in this place to realize that in the end, Shivaji will lose badly."

The man snorted, "What can someone like me do to him? After all, everyone here believes he is meant to be Emperor. Even the Gods have ordained it!"

"That damned sword! Ever since Shivaji got it, he has never lost a battle. Goddess Bhavani has made him invincible!" said the giant, eyes blazing with anger.

"At least, the people think so."

"You don't?" Ahmed asked.

The man shrugged and said, "Fine clothes can make one look like a King, and superstition can cause strange things to happen." He shot the giant a glance, before continuing, "I deal with Shivaji very often, and he certainly appears to be only flesh and blood to me."

"Really? You are part of the inner circle?" Ahmed stroked his beard.

Chuffed by the look of admiration on his new friend's face, the man threw caution to the wind and said, "Come to my house, we can talk freely there."

Lit up by flickering torches, the man could now see some grey hair in Ahmed's beard. As if his speech and facial hair weren't enough, there was a faint, sweet smell of perfume on him too. Was he one of Aurangzeb's men? The man realized he would have to be very careful. He offered Ahmed some water and fruits. "When did you enter Raigad? And how could you manage to go unnoticed? I heard no mention of a stranger in the marketplace."

Ahmed said with a chuckle, "It may be hard to believe, but I am light on my feet. I reached here last night with a group of shepherds, and since then I've been stealing scraps and hiding in the bushes. It was terribly hot in that thick, black shawl I used to cover myself, and my back is screaming from staying stooped over so they wouldn't notice my height." He leaned back against the wall as if he hadn't a care in the world.

The awkward silence was pierced by the loud wail of a crying child a few houses over. The man examined the stranger's face for a long time before he blurted out, "Are you a spy?"

"I travel far and wide in the service of my master. I seek only his happiness and continued prosperity."

The man stiffened and stood up. "I think you should go! I won't hand you over to the guards, but you can't stay here."

"What is it, my friend? Did I say something wrong?"

"You only talk in circles. I'm not happy where I am, but I have no wish to die a traitor. Please leave!"

Unperturbed, Ahmed met the man's gaze and nodded. "I'll come straight to the point. Shivaji has wronged you, and you want reparation for your losses. I need to stop the Coronation at any cost and convince the people that the Gods are angry with Shivaji!"

The man's dry laughter echoed in the room, and then he rasped, "Good luck with that! How can the Maratha people ever think he is not the greatest King ever! Even the mighty Aurangzeb, with all his horses, elephants, and men, could not hold Shivaji in one place for very long, and you… you want to stop the Coronation? Are you out of your mind?"

"I have a plan. We are going to steal the Bhavani Talwar!"

Chapter 7

May, 1674
Naikwadi

The epic Battle of Salher was talked about for years afterwards – how Prataprao Gujar had first attacked and then retreated as part of Shivaji's brilliant strategy; how Moropant Pingale had reached with 20,000 men and blocked in Ikhlas Khan's men, and how the valiant and clever Marathas had decimated the massive Mughal army. People told their grandchildren about the cloud of dust that covered the battlefield over many square miles – dust whipped up by the fighting soldiers, horses, camels, and elephants. The battle raged on for 12 hours and ended in a famous victory for the Marathas. Buoyed by their success, Shivaji Raje and his men then set about retaking many of their forts, and raiding and capturing territory after territory. Aurangzeb's soldiers had been thoroughly demoralized, and their leaders had been shaken and chastised. Finally, the land returned to peace.

"Sarjya! Where is that boy?"

Prajakta looked up from the *bhakri* she was making. "What is it, Baba?"

"*Aga,* he was supposed to bring me some honey from the forest. I need some to make an ointment for Lakshman's wound."

"The one he got with the *patta*?" Prajakta knew Lakshman was learning to use the broadsword in battle; he had been stoked to be one of the few men selected for the training.

"Hmm...," Baba said, his mind on other things. "I hope your brother hasn't landed in any trouble as usual. I'll go and ..."

"I'll go, Baba!" Prajakta quickly extinguished the fire. "You eat. Everything is ready. Aai will be back from the temple soon. I'll go look for Sarjya."

"And the honey!" Baba's voice followed her down the alley.

Once Prajakta exited the village, she heard the sound of metal on metal. The village men had cleared a patch of land near the main entrance to Naikwadi, and were using the area for practice. They were being trained in the use of the new Spanish blades – *Firangi,* they called them. Raje had decreed that all his men should use the new, improved swords, and the straight, double-edged blades, which most Marathas had never used, resulting in multiple cuts and injuries for the novice swordsmen. Prajakta lingered, watching the blades shine and shimmer as the rays of the morning sun hit the steel. The moving swords made silver arcs as they cut through the air in an intricate but deadly dance.

"Tai!" Sopan broke away from the group and ran to her.

"*Arre* Sopan, what are you doing over there? Don't tell me you are practising with them!" Pajakta glanced at the clashing, feinting men, then back at her friend. "You are just not old enough...," her voice trailed off as she realized Sopan had grown taller than her. *When did he grow so big? And were those muscles under that rolled-up sleeve?*

"Relax, Tai!" Sopan's soft voice eased her jangled nerves. "I'm nearly as large as some of the men, and strong too, thanks to all the hammering I do at my father's smithy. So, sometimes they call me to help them practise," he said, before pausing to wipe the trickle of sweat at his brow. "They say I'm built like one of the Pathans!"

Prajakta was still shaken by the realization that they were all growing up in the blink of an eye. The two of them watched the men practice; their yells, shouts of advice, and teasing provided entertainment for the watching villagers as well.

"That's a *patta*!" Sopan's voice rose in pitch. "I want to learn to use that one," he said and pointed.

The huge sword with the gauntlet had to have been built for a giant. Prajakta stole a glance at the young boy next to her – the chubby toddler who had played hide and seek with her, and the poet who wove dreams with words – and tried to reconcile that boy with the image of a warrior. She shook her head, failing to fuse the two. Maybe this time, there would be peace for many years, and all these boys would become old men before war broke out near them again. Aai Bhavani, she prayed, let that Aurangzeb sit happily in his palace, and never venture south again.

Sopan looked down at his arms and said, "I'm lifting weights too; I'm going to… I'm definitely going to fight with the *patta* one day!" He flashed a sudden smile. "Did Sarjya tell you we saw some French guns yesterday?"

Prajakta was jolted back to reality. "Guns? *Arre Deva*! Sarjya didn't touch them, did he? Did he steal one? Did you count them properly?" She knew their King had ordered small and large guns, along with lead, from the French factory at Rajapur, and that the English were not happy with the growing co-operation between the Maratha King and the French.

Sopan chortled. "No, we didn't even go close to them! They were in a box being transported to Raigad on their way from Pune. My Baba just pointed them out," he broke off after a shout from the men. "I have to go back. Tell Sarjya I'll meet him tonight."

"But, but…," Prajakta sputtered. "Do you know where he is?" she shouted.

"He went to the forest about an hour ago!" came the faint reply.

Muttering to herself, Prajakta turned for the forest outside the village when she bumped into someone. "Ohhh!"

"Ouch! Tai, why are you speaking to yourself?"

"Woof, woof!" Kaloo danced excitedly around his favourite two people, pretending to nip their ankles.

"Stop, stop it, Kaloo!" Sarjya yelled. "You'll make me drop the honeycomb! Oof, why did you cuff me, Tai?"

"You… you silly boy! Where were you? Baba needed that honey urgently." Prajakta grasped his arm and pulled him closer. She drew back in surprise, then touched Sarjya's swollen right cheek, tsk tsking as he winced. "Baba told you to cover your face, *na re*?"

"I did! I used my cummerbund, but the damn thing fell off when I was climbing the tree, so I thought-" Sarjya took a look at his sister's face and decided not to continue his story; he quickly changed the subject, saying, "Look Tai, I got bit behind my ear also!"

That night, after they had eaten a hearty meal, Ganya came over. Sarjya spat out the peanut shell he was eating and said, "*Kay re* Ganya? I've been observing you for many days – your clothes are totally different now – white and grey, ugh! Did all your bright clothes float away in the river when your mother was washing them, or did the colour fade with time?" He tugged Ganya's sleeve. "Are you wearing your father's kurta and leggings?"

"Yes, I noticed the change too." Prajkata said. "And you've become so thin! Are you eating properly? Do your old clothes not fit you now?"

"I've also been wanting to ask this," Sopan arrived just in time to say.

They all turned to stare at their friend, who remained unusually quiet. Prajakta shot an inquiring glance at Sopan; he shook his head and shrugged.

"What is it, Ganya? Is something wrong?" Prajakta whispered.

As if on cue, Kaloo crawled over to him, whimpering as he licked Ganya's feet. Silence filled the air as the children waited for the usually boisterous boy to answer. The fragrance of jasmine arose from Malhar Kaku's courtyard and scented the night, as if trying to ease the tense moment.

Ganya blinked a couple of times before looking up at his concerned friends. "I'm trying to become…to act more… normal! I just…"

Sarjya's forehead was a web of questions. Prajakta and Sopan looked at each other again.

"Tell us *na*, Ganya, what has happened to you? What do you mean by normal? Did someone say something to you?" Prajakta asked softly.

The boy stared at his feet for a long time; then he squatted, and the others did the same. They watched his lips quiver with strong emotion and willed him to speak. What was it that had disturbed him? They all missed their loud, colourful friend, the heart and soul of their gang. His ready wit and sense of humour brought so much joy to their lives. "I…I want to be like you!" Ganya blurted out. "I mean… I don't… I don't want to stand out and have others mock... er …notice me."

"But that was the whole point! You wanted to be different," Sarjya almost yelled.

"No, I don't!" Ganya's eyes flashed. "Well, not anymore," he whispered.

Prajakta sighed and shifted closer to him. "Ganya," she faltered, then began again, "we all love your style and your uniqueness; why would you want to change and become like someone else?"

"But Tai, they call me *Vidushak*!" came the anguished reply. He stroked Kaloo's head and smiled at the dog before saying, "You all are my friends; when you tease me, I know it's in jest. But, when they… the village boys and even men look at me, they jeer my weight, and my love of mimicry. They tell me to join the troop of dancers that tours the state. They say…," he said, his fingers tightening on Kaloo's ear, and the dog squealed and moved away to Sarjya. "Sorry, Kaloo!" Ganya's eyes filled with tears. He hastily stood up. "I'll talk to you all later; it's getting late, and my father needs something."

The three friends watched him scurry away in the moonlight. His palpable sadness had affected them all; even Sarjya was at a loss for words.

"Children," the three turned as Baba walked over to them, rubbing his fingers free of the gooey yellow paste he had been making, "I heard some of what Ganya had to say…"

"Baba, what should we do now? He's almost become a different person – such a sad, scared little boy, dragging his feet and hiding in the shadows. What could be going on in his mind? How can we help him deal with this?" Prajakta asked.

Her father's gentle smile was like a balm for their souls. "Don't worry, he'll be fine. After all, he has the three of you. You all are at that vulnerable age when people's opinions begin to matter more than your own, and doubts creep in about how you look. Just keep reminding him he's your friend, no matter what. Show Ganya how much you value him and need him around."

Chapter 8

From Maloji, the village headman's house to the minuscule hut occupied by the widowed Manda Ajji and her nasty black cat; from the oldest Naikwadi resident, the doddering Kanoji *Panjoba,* to the only just learning to speak Sai – they were all talking about only one thing – the Grand Coronation!

"I heard they are expecting a hundred thousand guests at Raigad. Is that true?" Parvati, the headman's wife, asked.

"How should I know?" Maloji said, moustache quivering, "As if I have been called!"

"Hmm, no one we know has got an invitation," Parvati said, pursing her lips. "I'd give anything to be able to take a look inside. They say a whole new palace is being built – with a Grand Darbar Hall that has massive golden pillars and a massive throne for our King!"

"I'm sure we will all hear about the ceremony a few weeks later," the headman said with a shrug.

"How can you be so dispassionate about it? Maybe they'll call the headmen of all the villages!" His wife's face lit up.

Maloji looked at her and sighed. "Let's see."

Hanumanta was hard at work in his smithy; he had a fresh batch of swords to finish. The Spanish blades had been delivered the previous evening, and he needed to fashion the knuckle-guards and grips perfectly. He had warned the Subhedar that the grips he could make would be very basic, and that they shouldn't expect any fine work.

The man had laughed before replying, "We'll tell the nobles and ministers to send their swords to a goldsmith!" Hanumanta slipped off the kurta that was plastered to his back with sweat. His muscles glistening, he hammered the steel, his mind on all the intricate designs the goldsmiths would make. A twinge of regret arose at the fact that Naikwadi had no goldsmith, and the women would go to Pune for all their needs. Then he shrugged – their village was too small for such a skilled person to set up shop, and most of his people possessed no gold anyway. But, after the massacre by Diler Khan, no adult man was left alive in Pune, and so, every week, some woman would try to ask him for help.

"Do you know anyone in the area who can repair my earrings? They are very old; my mother-in-law gave them to me. She is coming over next week and will insist that I wear them!" Lakshman's worried wife, Sona, said, "Or maybe you can do it?"

"*Nahin ga pori,*" Hanumanta wiped his brow and smiled, softly adding, "I can't do such delicate work! I know someone in Bhor, but most of the skilled artisans have been summoned to Raigad."

"For the Coronation? I heard the throne will be made of solid gold!" Sona's eyes widened. She sighed at her tiny hoops and said, "I guess I'll just have to face my mother-in-law's scolding for my poor handling of her precious gift."

Sopan came in with a bucket of water just as she was leaving, and some sloshed onto the workshop floor. "Oops, sorry Baba!" he said, with a curious look at the departing woman. "What's up with her? She looked upset."

"She needed me to be a goldsmith!" Hanumanta ran his fingers over his head and smiled at his son. "Maybe I should learn some of that – you know, with the decorative knuckle-guards, sheaths and hilts to go with the swords?"

Father and son looked down at their large hands and stubby fingers, then at each other, and guffawed together. *Naah!*

"But seriously, Baba, have you ever seen the Bhavani Sword – I mean, up close? Does it really have diamonds and rubies?"

"When I last saw Raje was the same time as you, son; and that was when he visited our village. The sword was sheathed and by his side, and I didn't really pay much attention then. But yesterday, Tuka showed me a scroll painting he wants to give Aaisaheb at the Coronation; he's painted a life-sized Shivaji Raje with his sword – that one has emeralds and diamonds too."

"Tuka has been invited to Raigad for the Coronation?" Sopan asked.

"*Nahin re*. He told me, if they call him, he wants to have a gift ready for our Queen Mother!" Hanumanta shook his head and said, "As if people like us will ever get to go there!"

"If Tanaji were still alive, he'd call us!"

"Sarjya?" Sopan turned at the statement. "When did you come?"

"I was just… er… passing by…," Sarjya looked at Hanu Kaka and faltered.

"Were you practising your spy skills?"

Sarja waited for the reprimand; when he realized he wasn't about to be scolded, he grinned. "Yes, actually, I followed Sopan back here, as silent as his shadow! Then I began listening through the roof…"

Father and son looked up at the thatched roof of the workshop, aghast.

"But, forget about that," Sarjya rushed to speak, "what I wanted to say was that if Tanaji were still alive, he'd definitely want us to be at the

Coronation, right, Sopan? After all, we were his little friends, as he used to say."

Sopan nodded. "He was a great man, and gave the greatest sacrifice for us all."

All three of them sighed. There was silence for a while, then Sopan turned to speak, "But Sarjya..." he gasped. There was no one there! "Where did he go?"

Hanumanta chuckled. "That boy is getting good!"

Sarjya raced home; he had forgotten the time again! It was getting late, and the cows needed to be milked – Aai would be furious. He entered the courtyard expecting smouldering glances, but his mother was chatting with two other women and didn't even notice him.

"Really? *Tuladaan*?" Savitri said. "I've only heard about it, never saw anyone doing it. Wasn't Lord Ram weighed in gold when he came back to Ayodhya?"

"As if our Shivaji Raje is any less than a God for us!"

Sarjya bit his tongue, but the woman in the green saree had already turned around at his words. Maloji Kaka's wife, Parvati! He drew back into the shadows – she had a very sharp tongue, especially when it came to their gang of four – he was sure it was because she felt envious that Raje had praised them, and because they had got to meet Aaisaheb, while her husband, the headman, remained out of the limelight. Parvati Kaku was always brimming with gossip, not only from Naikwadi but also from the surrounding villages.

Baba emerged from his experimental workshop, his hands covered in purple goo. He ducked, hoping the women wouldn't notice him as he tiptoed towards the door. Sarjya grinned at him, then turned to listen to the women talk.

"So, will the priest weigh our King in gold?" Aai asked.

"Not only that," Parvati replied, "they'll also weigh him in silver, ghee, copper, iron, cloth, fruits, spices and sugar too!"

The three women stared at each other excitedly. What an amazing sight that would be!

Parvati Kaku continued, "And there will be an awning of golden cloth, and draperies of richly embroidered satin cloth!"

Malhar Kaku snorted. "They'd better keep that Ganya away or else, he'll cut the cloth to make kurtas for himself!"

Sarjya stepped forward, fire burning in his eyes. "Ganya is not a thief! Why will he use Shivaji Raje's curtains for himself?" Glaring at the three women, he said, "And so what if he likes rich colourful stuff? What's the harm? Does he have to become part of the jungle or the soil by wearing only drab clothes?"

Aai looked at his trembling lips and clenched fists. "*Nahi re bala,* we didn't say it was wrong. He's just so different..."

Sarjya didn't wait to hear the rest of her words; he yelled, "I've milked the cows, and now I'm going," before stomping away. *What was so bad about being different?*

"What's happened, Aai?" Prajakta came out of the kitchen, her hands still coated with flour. "Was that Sarjya? Why was he yelling?"

Parvati Kaku stood up, dusted her sari, and said, "You have spoiled your children, Savitri! They behave like adults, that too rude ones." She glared at Prajakta. "One is too high and mighty to behave like other girls, and the other is rude and refuses to show elders any respect!"

Aai saw Prajakta about to open her mouth, and rushed in to speak, "*Aho,* Parvati Tai, it's not like that at all..." Whatever she was going to say died on her lips as a shadow darkened the doorway; it was two men – Mavalas with red turbans – tall and stern looking.

"Is this Mahadev Naik's house?" one of the men asked.

"Yes," Prajakta stepped forward and answered, just as Baba emerged from inside.

"Are you Prajakta?"

"Yes... and you are?"

"We have come from Raigad. Aaisaheb has sent us!" the man said, beaming with pride.

Aai moved to stand behind Prajakta and clutched her shoulders tightly. Parvati Kaku and Malhar Kaku stood there in amazement, their mouths open.

"Tai...the villagers said some men-" Sarjya screeched to a halt at the sight of the men.

"As we were saying," the Mavala continued, "Aaisaheb requests the presence of Prajakta, Sarjya, Ganya and Sopan at Raigad as soon as possible."

All the women gasped again. "Have they been called for the Coronation?" Parvati Kaku was the first to speak. She has the strangest expression on her face, Prajakta thought, almost as if she's angry at the news.

Malhar Kaku was eager to ask, "But the ceremony is weeks away! What will they do there so early?"

Baba raised his hand to silence the two women, "Let him continue please. *Bhau*, what else do you know?"

"We were told only to bring the children back with us as soon as we could; that's all. Aaisaheb said specifically to tell their parents it may be a while till they return, and that she will take good care of them." The man turned to Baba and added, "Some more men with horses are with us. We are camping near the entrance to the village tonight, and we'll leave with the children tomorrow morning."

Chapter 9

"Did you see Parvati Kaku's face?" Sarjya licked his fingers clean of the last morsel of *varan bhaat,* then gave Prajakta a dreamy smile and leaned back against the wall. "I'm full!"

Aai beamed at him; her baby boy was growing so fast. She blinked rapidly to dismiss the welling tears of pride, then reminded herself to get him a black thread to ward off the evil eye, especially since the last visual she had of the headman's wife was one of shock, jealousy and bitterness seeping from her sickly smile.

'*Wah Wah, masta ahe*! Your children will go to Raigad, little nobles that they are!' Parvati had said before she walked away, muttering something about having a lot to do at home.

Sarjya turned to watch his mother pick up Baba's plate, then looked down at his sister's fingers making patterns in her plate. She had been unusually quiet. "What is it, Tai? Aren't you happy we're going to meet Aaisaheb again?"

"Don't you want to go?" Baba's knees creaked as he sat down after washing his hands.

Prajakta shook her head, then met his eyes with a reassuring look and said, "I was just wondering why we've been called. What could have happened in Raigad? There are so many people there – warriors, spies, administrators – how can we be of any use there? And... and there's still some time for the Coronation, so it's not for that."

"*Beta,* let's cross the bridge when we come to it. Why are you anticipating things in advance? First, enjoy the travel, go there, listen to their story and then react. It's of no use to think of a hundred possibilities, all of which may be wrong. Rest your mind and body for the journey ahead, and whatever task our Queen Mother has in mind for you." He shifted closer and rubbed his finger on her furrowed forehead gently before saying, "You worry too much, child!"

"*Bagha na,* she'll get wrinkles at this age only!" Aai shouted from inside. "Then who will marry her?"

Before Prajakta could react, Sarjya moved to get up and dropped his plate with a clang. He stuck out his tongue, "Oops! Wasn't it good that I had licked it clean? Nothing left to spill!" They all laughed loudly, and Prajakta felt her mind empty of both, the anger and the useless worrying. Trust her brother to make them smile in every situation!

"You're home early!" Sopan walked into their home to find his father squatting on the floor. "I was going to make the *varan* …I thought…"

"Don't fret, son," Hanumanta said, stirring the bubbling lentils. He smacked his lips as the fragrance wafted through their home. "I wanted to eat with you – you're leaving early tomorrow, and it may be a while before you're back." The gentle giant smiled lovingly at his son and said, "Come, sit down. Have you washed up?"

"Yes, Baba," Sopan blinked before speaking. "Are you… will you … how will you manage alone?" he finally blurted out.

The man chuckled. "Like I did when you were a baby! The people of Naikwadi always step up. Savitri Tai has already made me promise to go over to their place for every meal – she was most insistent, even waggled her finger in my face!"

Sopan stirred the *varan* into the rice. "We are all like one large family here in Naikwadi. But still, won't you feel lonely without me?"

"Of course, I will miss you, son, that's for sure. But don't worry, I have enough work to stay busy. You just enjoy the stay at Raigad, and whatever our Queen Mother needs your help for, do your best to achieve that. That reminds me.... here!" Hanumanta turned to a small bundle by his side and said, "Take this with you and give it to Aaisaheb; one shouldn't go empty-handed."

"What is it, Baba?"

"A small *katyar* for her! Made with the same firangi blade the Mavalas are now using. Our Queen is also a warrior; maybe she'll carry it with her for protection."

Sopan's eyes shone. "What a marvellous idea!" He sat up straighter, proud of his father's skills

***

Sniff!

Ganya's mother wiped her eyes with her padar and nudged her husband, who was staring blankly into space.

"Huh?" He looked at his wife, then at his son.

"*Aho,* say something!" his wife urged.

"Must you go?" the man asked.

"Of course not, Baba. If you need me to stay, I won't go." Ganya's drawn face was telling a different story.

"*Aho,* what are you saying?" his wife hissed. "This is such a great opportunity for our son to go to Raigad for the Coronation; no one in our village has even been invited!"

"It's not exactly...," Ganya ventured.

"And do you know they will be taken care of by Aaisaheb herself! You also *na,* think only of yourself. Already behaving like an old man!

Nothing will happen if you have to work a little extra in the fields for some days."

Ganya's father shut his eyes wearily and said, "Whatever you say, dear."

"How many clothes should I pack?" she continued. "Nowadays, you don't wear that red shirt you used to love. What happened? Did it tear?"

***

Even though it was only dawn, half of Naikwadi seemed to have gathered to say goodbye to the gang. Bundles of clothing, food, and small gifts were loaded rapidly, followed by the dog, and finally the excited children. As they waved to their parents, Prajakta and Sarjya were reminded of their time at Sangamner, how desperately they had wanted to get away from home, only to end up begging to go back. Sarjya elbowed his sister and pointed to Ganya, who was pretending to sleep. "People want him to become a *Vidushak*; look, he's such a bad actor, he can't even pretend to be asleep."

"Of course not, I'm a great actor!" the boy answered, then bit his lip.

They all laughed. Sopan nudged Sarjya and said, "At least for this journey, you are an invited guest, not a stowaway!" He winked at Ganya to make him smile. "Did I ever tell you the story of Ashok, the master of disguise?"

"No!" they all chorused.

Amid laughter, stories and food, the journey of 12 hours went by in no time. It was dark by the time the horses made the steep climb up to the massive Raigad Fort, but their arrival was eagerly awaited. Among those who waited for the children with lanterns was a familiar face.

"Rama Tai!" Prajakta exclaimed. She had met the beautiful woman only once before, years ago, when they had helped Tanaji, but she still secretly aspired to be as graceful as her.

"Welcome, Prajakta!" Rama hugged her and smiled at the boys. "Welcome, all of you! You must be tired and hungry too. Come!"

They quickly washed their hands and feet and sat down to eat. Sarjya looked around at the massive room where women were carrying in vegetables and fruits and taking out used utensils. "Does everyone in the fort eat here?"

"Yes, Sarjya, we all sit here for our meals now. Hundreds of people are here for the preparations – labourers, carpenters, tailors, masons – so cooking is done in the next room on a huge scale, and this is our dining area. The artisans have all eaten long ago, and possibly even slept."

Ganya licked his fingers and gave her a shy smile before asking, "Will we get to watch all the arrangements for the Coronation?"

"Of course!" Rama ladled another helping of kheer into all their bowls despite their protests.

"Have more," she said. "You need strength; you are all still growing."

"Some more than others!" Sarjya looked pointedly at Ganya and sniggered. "What?" he asked Prajakta, who dug her elbows into his side. "He is getting fat, only not tall!"

"Shut up, Sarjya, can't you see he's hurt?" she hissed.

"*Arre*, he knows I'm only teasing." Sarjya bent to try to look into Ganya's eyes. "Hey brother, look at me! Sorry, I was just joking. You've actually become much thinner. Are your eyes wet?"

"It's ok," Ganya whispered, but his lips trembled.

Prajakta and Sopan exchanged glances; they really needed to get Ganya to talk openly with them. He was never to be this sensitive; he'd laugh off their teasing, even retort by mocking them in turn for their bland ways. What on earth had happened to him?

Sarjya patted his stomach and said, "The food was amazing, Rama Tai! Does everyone here eat this well?"

Rama smiled, "Aaisaheb always says quality work needs quality food. And now we need to go and meet her."

Prajakta goggled. "Now? This late?"

"Yes, she is waiting for you!"

The Queen Mother had stayed up and was waiting to speak to them at this time of the night? It must be something hugely important that she had to tell them. Sarjya's eyes gleamed. Time to finally find out the secret behind their invitation here!

They quickly walked past the sleeping labourers to the central courtyard, and then into the Rani Mahal and up the winding steps. The hissing and spitting noises from the flickering torches on the dark stone walls were the only sounds the children heard as they climbed the two floors to the Queen Mother's room.

Sopan glanced at the guards guarding the simple wooden door to the entrance. They stared down at the children with impassive faces; then, at a nod from Rama, they uncrossed their lances and permitted them all to enter. The room was nearly the size of their entire home, but it was simply decorated. Carved wooden pillars supported the high walls, and the wooden shutters on the windows overlooking the courtyard had been thrown open; Prajakta could hear the laughter of a few late workers as they made their way to bed. A beautiful silver lamp shone from a corner of the room, and the torches illuminated the smile on the regal old Queen's face. Prajakta was surprised to find her alone. No ladies in waiting.

"Welcome, children!" Aaisaheb beckoned them closer. "I hope you had a pleasant journey."

"Yes, thank you!" they chorused and fell silent.

Aaisaheb met their curious glances one by one, and her expression became serious. "It's late, so I'll get straight to the point," she said. "I need you to solve a mystery; there's been a theft here!"

Chapter 10

Aaisaheb nodded wryly at their flabbergasted expressions; it was time to tell them the devastating news. She spoke softly, "It's like this… three days ago, someone stole a large emerald, a giant ruby and 11 small diamonds from the Bhavani Sword!"

Prajakta gasped. The sheer effrontery of this thief – no one would dare even touch Raje's sacred sword – and to actually remove the precious jewels… it was as if someone had gouged out the eye of an idol! Her chest heaved at the news, but the foreboding expression on the Queen Mother's face made her choke down her sobs. She turned to Sarjya, who was shaking his head in disbelief, and to Sopan and Ganya, who were looking at her, dumbstruck.

Aaisaheb sighed and continued, "It happened four days ago; Shivba is sure the jewels were there at the time he returned from his evening rounds. Then, he had a few meetings and slept. The next afternoon, when he was dressing for an audience with some villagers, he noticed the Bhavani Talwar was unsheathed." Her breath hitched, and she took time to compose herself before saying, "When he lifted the sword, he noted the missing jewels. During a search of the room, the sheath was discovered; it had been tossed below his bed."

"The sword," Prajakta asked, "we've heard it has many jewels. Were only these missing?"

"Yes, 11 small ones, and two large stones – 13 jewels were taken in all. There were many more diamonds, and some other smaller emeralds too, but for some reason that... that traitor took only those."

The silence that followed was punctuated only by the chirping of the crickets outside. Then, Aaisaheb stood up with a rustle of silks and said, "I am leaving tomorrow to oversee some preparations, so I needed to speak to you all tonight. Raje's trusted personal aide, Tukoji, will take you tomorrow to the royal chambers and show you exactly where the sword was and who all had access to the rooms."

"My dear children," her concerned eyes met each of theirs in turn as she spoke, "you are a brave and intelligent group who can ask questions and move around without appearing to be a threat to anyone. Hopefully, they have not yet left the Fort's premises, and your sleuthing can help us identify this miscreant. Only a few of us, and now you, know about the missing jewels. You have to keep this a secret. We are telling people that I have invited you for a few days to discuss a small entertainment performance for the King's Coronation; please act accordingly. I trust you will protect this information with your life." The lines around Aaisaheb's eyes grew deeper with every word she spoke. She turned wearily to Rama, who muttered, 'I'll show you to your rooms, children,' and ushered them out before they could say another word.

***

"Burrp!" Sarjya covered his mouth and looked at the other three. "Sorry, over ate!"

"As usual! You can eat at any time of the day or night!" Prajakta smiled and said, "And you tease Ganya about his eating!" She looked around at the boys' room; it was a large one with only the three beds for

Sopan, Ganya and Sarjya. Her own solo room adjoined theirs, though she would have preferred to be with them all. It was after midnight; Rama had bid them a hasty goodnight and rushed home, but they were all wide awake now. Aaisaheb's unbelievable announcement had raised innumerable questions in their minds, and there was just no way they could wait till morning to discuss it all.

"Tai, tomorrow we'll finally get to see and touch the Bhavani Talwar!"

Prajakta sighed, "That's the first thing you want to mention, Sarjya?"

"No, of course not! I just… I mean…," he said, his eyes lighting up, "it's the Bhavani Talwar!" Prajakta understood his awe; the magical sword was the subject of legends, and was inevitably mentioned every time Raje's name was spoken in any village in Maharashtra – after all, Goddess Bhavani herself had bestowed it on their King. But for Sarjya, the weapon was a revered object – he worshipped Shivaji Raje – in fact, he had insisted on placing a small statue of the King with the Gods and Goddesses Aai anointed and prayed to each day. To be this close to Shivaji's famous sword, and possibly actually hold it in his mere mortal hands was a dream come true. But they all had to set aside their excitement and get serious about why they had been summoned there.

"We have to think of a skill too, so we have something to pretend to do when people ask us," Ganya said, wriggling with excitement. "We can enact one of Sopan's stories! Do you remember the one about the four friends who ride out in different directions to meet their destinies? I'll make the sounds of the horses, and maybe they'll give us some costumes too." His face lit up at the thought.

Prajakta rolled her eyes. This one had totally different priorities!

Ganya caught her look and rushed to add, "Of course, first we should learn all about the dastardly theft. But what I don't understand is, Raje has a fabulous network of spies and warriors, and still they called us here?" He pulled at a loose thread on his kurta. "What can we do if they fail?"

Sarjya glared at him, but Prajakta tugged at his elbow and silenced her brother. "No one has failed, Ganya. It's just been three days. Aaisaheb wants to cover all the possible gaps and ensure the jewels and the thief are found as soon as possible; after all, time is short."

"Why can't they send messengers to all corners of the kingdom and announce a large reward? I'm sure if all our people are on the alert, that evil man will be found in no time!" Sarjya said.

Sopan shook his head at his words. "*Arre* Sarjya, they don't want the news to become public knowledge."

"But why?" Ganya and Sarjya spoke together.

"Because it's a sensitive matter," Prajakta looked around and lowered her voice. "The lesser people who know, the better. One, because there may be a panic situation among the people, like the time when Aurangzeb's men looted Kashi and Afzal Khan desecrated Tuljapur. The Bhavani Sword has godlike status in people's minds, and knowing it has been damaged may lower morale, especially at a time when peace has come to us after so much sacrifice. So, if the Royal Family continues their normal routine as if nothing has happened, the population will go about their daily work routine calmly, and the thief will begin to wonder what went wrong."

"Yes, Tai," Sopan added, "If they aimed at creating an obstacle to the Coronation and things continue to move smoothly, they might try something else and make a mistake."

"Another reason it might be better not to tell people," Prajakta said, "is that if the thief plans to sell the jewels for money, he will be more relaxed if he believes the theft has not been discovered yet, or that most people don't know."

"Yes, Tai, he may become careless!" Ganya sat up straighter.

"Exactly!" a grinning Prajakta said, "So we keep things to ourselves and talk to only each other and Rama, and this Tukoji, whom we will meet tomorrow. We have to try and understand exactly how the theft took place and who the people behind it are." She frowned and said, "Remember when Sarjya went missing… how we all got scared and were unable to think clearly for a while?"

"And then everyone in Naikwadi came together, and we kept thinking of ideas!" Sopan continued.

"And the wrong ideas failed, but they helped us reach the correct one!" Ganya stood up and whooped for joy, setting Kaloo off.

The excited shouts and barking were allowed to go on for only a brief while before the other three hastily shut them down.

"It's late," Prajakta whispered, "you'll wake up everyone!"

"Except the thief!" Sarjya giggled.

"As if he is waiting around now! He has possibly reached Agra by now," Sopan said.

"Really, Sopan? You think it's the Mughals who have carried out this plot?" Ganya's face fell. "But what will Aurangzeb do with more jewels? Surely, he has thousands more; he can probably swim in the huge stack he owns!"

Prajakta's plaits flew as she shook her head and laughed.

"Why are you all laughing?" came the hurt question.

"*Arre* Ganya, who is our Raje's sworn enemy? Who is likely not to want the Coronation to go ahead smoothly?"

Ganya's eyes grew moon-sized, then he blurted out, "Oh, now I understand! It's not about the jewels."

"That's just one possibility, Ganya," Sopan put his hand around his friend's shoulders and said, "our King has multiple enemies, external and internal, and we need to consider them all."

A mystery! Sarjya vibrated with excitement, making Kaloo's tail wag furiously.

"What Sopan is saying is perfectly correct, and we don't know so much of the political situation; the news that reaches our villages and then is allowed to filter down to us children is only a small part of the actual story." Prajakta grew serious as she continued, "We will need to ask many more questions and come up with possible suspects."

"Like when we thought the Mughals stole the treasure we found in that cave, but actually it was that scar-faced man?" Ganya asked.

Prajakta darted a quick glance at Sarjya; she knew he still had nightmares from the time the villain had kidnapped him at the Dussehra festivities. He gulped once, then agreed, "Yes, we should make a list of all possible people who would want to steal the jewels."

A huge clatter from the courtyard made them jump. Sarjya ran to the window to check. "Just someone dropping a gigantic brass pot. Good thing there wasn't any food in it – so much would have gone waste!" he told them.

"There will be full pots tomorrow! *Chala* boys!" Prajakta clapped her hands together softly and laughed at the woof from Kaloo, "and dog too! Go to sleep now, we need to wake up bright and early tomorrow and get to work right away."

"But you better not solve the mystery tomorrow itself," Sarjya whispered to her at the door.

"Why Sarjya?"

"*Aga* Tai, I want to be here for the Coronation – and that's two weeks away. So, take your time, think slowly!" he said, giggling at her aghast expression. "I'm joking, just joking!" *Maybe,* he whispered to himself.

Chapter 11

"No, no, just a few moments more!" Sarjya's eyes were screwed tightly shut as if to deny entry to the early morning sun.

"*Chal re, ooth*!" Prajakta shook him gently, then with more force. "We have been called here for an important task, not to laze around."

"Just a little more sleep," he pleaded.

"Sarjya, get up! Ganya and Sopan are already bathed and ready!"

Sarjya opened one eye and groaned. He dragged himself off the mattress and trudged to the courtyard, where Prajakta had kept a bucket of water and some ash ready for cleaning. The other two boys thoroughly enjoyed his complaining commentary as they waited for him to finish. Then, they all raced to the dining hall and gulped down piping hot *sheera* with milk.

***

"Are you ready, children?"

The voice was feminine, but when they looked up, the children saw a short, dark man standing over them, his lean face looking totally incongruous with the immense moustache he sported. Sarjya sniggered, then coughed to mask it. The milk he had been drinking entered the wrong tract, sending him into a coughing fit. Prajakta thumped him hard on his back.

"Ow!"

She glared at him and hissed, "Behave!"

Sarjya turned to the man, then nearly burst out laughing again. He pressed his lips together, wiped his mouth and hurried off muttering, "I have to wash the milk off my clothes."

The man shifted from foot to foot as he waited for the boy to return. "Done?" he asked. Prajakta gulped and shut her eyes, her body shaking as she now struggled not to laugh. The man's high-pitched, almost girlish voice had come as a total surprise to the children. The dark man sniffed and said, "I am Tukoji Shelar, personal aide to Shivaji Raje. Aaisaheb has asked me to show you Raje's chambers. Come!" He turned and marched out of the room, leaving them to scramble behind him, still covering their chuckles with their hands.

As a red-faced Tukoji climbed up the winding stone steps leading them deeper into the fort, Prajakta ran her fingers over the black rocks that made up the walls. They were designed to withstand a battering, she thought, but not from an enemy already inside. Who could have dared to touch their King's sword? Tukoji led them past halls and rooms – some with no doors at all, and some with barred ones; he stopped outside two rather imposing wooden doors with spikes on them.

"This must be Raje's room!" Sarjya whispered, his eyes shining with excitement.

Prajakta looked at the two strapping guards who stood on either side, shining spears in hand. At a nod from Tukoji, the men stepped aside and pushed open the door. Would their King be inside, Prajakta wondered, then shook her head. Of course not! He was rumoured to get up at the crack of dawn to pray and exercise.

Sarjya stepped inside, and his eyes popped out of his head. A..ma..

zing! Sarjya Naik was inside the chambers of his idol, his hero, Shivaji Raje! He turned around to take in the whole place, pinching himself to make sure he wasn't dreaming. The outer room was sparsely furnished; it had only a rug and a low table with scrolls.

"Must be maps or attack plans," Sopan whispered before they were led into the next room, which had a low bed and silk draperies.

Prajakta looked at the gleam in her brother's eyes and held on tightly to his hand, warning, "No, you can't lie down on the bed to experience how the King sleeps!"

He grinned at the expression on her face. *Maybe later,* he promised himself.

A large dressing room opened onto the bedroom, as did another room, this one with armours, shields and other fighting equipment. All four children inhaled sharply; this was the room where the swords were housed!

Sarjya looked around and asked, "There are no swords here, where are they?"

Tukoji's face was a stony mask; only his moustache moved as he spoke, "We have moved them to a secure location. The Bhavani Talwar will be shown to you later on," his moustache drooped as he continued, "in its present condition."

Sopan stepped forward to point out, "The person who stole the jewels would have to walk past the guards, into the bedroom and then into the weapons room."

Tukoji nodded glumly.

"And the guards are here all the time?" Prajakta asked.

"Every moment of every day," Shivaji's aide said with a sigh.

The children shook their heads – how could anyone have stolen the jewels from such a heavily guarded place? Only a magician could have done it!

"What is it, Kaloo?" Sarjya turned to the dog, who was sniffing in a corner of the bedroom. He turned around two or three times, then wagged his tail and barked. "What do you smell, boy?" Sarjya asked.

Keeping his nose to the ground, Kaloo moved to the other room, which housed the King's clothes and accessories. He pushed his head behind one of the cupboards and sneezed. Sopan and Sarjya moved together to pull the cupboard forward, then stepped back to find out what had excited Kaloo. It was a small mogra flower.

Tukoji bent to pick it up and frowned. "The only females permitted to enter here are Aaisaheb and Soyarabai, and neither of them wears flowers in their hair; besides, this flower hasn't wilted yet… must have fallen here recently. A woman!" Tukoji scratched his head and remarked, "Strange!"

"Maybe it's someone who cleans the room?" Prajakta asked.

"Or a maid who brought in some washed clothes or a message?" Sopan added.

Tukoki shook his head. "No one but the Queen brings up Raje's clothes or touches his necklaces and *pagadis*… and the attendant who cleans the rooms and maintains the sheets, curtains, etc., he's been with the King for 10 years, I trust him with my life. And he's a man!" He frowned, his forehead a deep web of lines.

They all stood there in silence for a while, pondering the matter. Prajakta sniffed, then moved to the weapons room again and sniffed again. She walked back to where the other stood, "Did any of you smell something sweet in that room?"

Sarjya rolled his eyes. "Of course we did; it was the mogra!"

"No, no, this is a different smell, Sarjya," she said, "something like the sandalwood paste Aai uses to anoint the gods on festivals, but more sickly-sweet."

Tukoji dashed to the weapons room, then turned from the doorway, his face a thunderous shade, "It's *attar*! How did I not smell it before?"

"Did many people enter the room since then?" Prajakta asked.

"We sealed the room immediately after the theft was discovered, and opened it only now to show you. That's why the smell is more intense now." Tukoji's eyes lit up with a host of possibilities. "*Attar*!" he whispered.

"*Attar*?" Ganya squeaked. "Don't Mughals use it? We've solved the case – Aurangzeb is behind the theft!"

"Many Muslim men do like to use the scent." Tukoji cleared his throat, "Could be anyone really, though Raje does have some Muslims among his trusted people."

"So, it could be a known person or someone totally new. Or someone wanting to convince us it's a Muslim." Prajakta looked at the now sombre man, watching with fascination at the way his nostrils flared and made his moustache quiver.

Tukoji took a deep breath before speaking, "In the last four days, that is, since the day prior to the theft, Raje had only one meeting here. We checked the homes of everyone who attended the meeting after the theft was discovered. I don't.... let me get that list again."

"Kaka, we also need a list of everyone who set foot inside Raje's chambers since the sword was last seen intact, even the names of all the guards on duty since that day."

Tukoji gave her a mocking smile before speaking, "You children think we didn't think of that already? Our King has a whole ministry of brilliant minds to strategize and investigate!"

"Then why..." Sarjya began.

"What we mean to say," Prajakta said, stepping in front of the bristling boy with a smile, "is that please could we have that list?"

"I will go get it," Tukoji strode to the door; then he turned back to glare at them. "Don't touch anything!" He exited, aware of the mutinous looks on their faces.

"That man hates us for no reason. We will find the missing jewels in one day itself, then they'll learn how smart we are!" Sarjya continued shooting imaginary daggers with his eyes.

"Where are you going?" Sopan shouted, and they all turned to catch Ganya edging closer to Raje's dressing room.

He gave them a sheepish smile and muttered, "Just looking at his clothes!"

The four of them stood in the doorway, admiring the contents of Shivaji's room. The simple white silks had inlays of gold and pearls, some of the cummerbunds were in bright colours, but by and large their King preferred white.

Ganya had a silly smile on his face, almost as if he had died and gone to heaven. Prajakta chortled at his wistful look. "Bright colours suit you more than whites, Ganya; they bring out the happiness inside you." She looked at his shy grin and said, "Keep smiling like this, ok? Mimic us all, dress in rainbow colours – stay just as you are!"

"Tai, do you think...," Sarjya began, then fell silent as Tukoji returned. "That was super-fast!" he mumbled, "must have sprinted back to make sure we didn't touch anything or even steal some new stuff!"

Kaloo growled in assent.

Tukoji offered the list to Sarjya, who stared blankly at the scroll, then passed it to Prajakta. "She reads better," he said, his cheeks dimpling in amusement at the astonished look on the man's face. Not many women or girls they knew could read.

All of them moved closer to listen to Prajakta read out the names on the scroll. "Monday evening after sunset – meeting with Raje in chambers. Seven present: Tukoji Naik," she glanced at the man in front of them, then continued, "Moropant Pingle, Vishnu Dhamal, Sonoji Gorpade, Hansaji Mohite, Mohammad Shaikh and Vitthoji Trimbak."

She went through the names of the guards, too, but there was no other Muslim name.

"So, Mohammed Shaikh," Tukoji's shoulders slumped as he spoke, "is the only one who could probably have worn *attar* openly. But it is possible the thief deliberately wore the scent to throw us off track," he sighed. "I've never noticed any strong scent on Shaikh, though, in all these years. And everyone present in that meeting was later summoned after the discovery of the theft, and they all volunteered to get their rooms checked – each one who was there that day, even the most trusted like Moropant, Raje's Peshwa and … and myself too, but nothing was found!"

"Hmm," Prajakta said, tapping her finger on the list as her mind raced furiously to connect the facts.

Chapter 12

"Kaka," Sopan began timidly, "if I may ask…it's a little silly but…"

"Speak up, child! We need to consider even the most minuscule of things." Even Tukoji's moustache seemed to sag with his shoulders.

"Did you… Was every room here… I mean, even the dressing room, the bedroom, and the outer hall, too, were searched? You know, just in case the jewels somehow became loose on their own and fell and rolled away?"

The man's chest rose and fell before he said, "Wishful thinking *pora*... if only that were the case! We combed the place from top to bottom for the stones. It was definitely intentional – the prising away of the emerald, ruby and diamonds – and the theft."

"So, before the meeting, Raje had been somewhere else?" Prajakta asked.

"Yes, he had been taking a tour of the fort and overseeing the preparations for the Coronation, but he had been carrying the Bhavani Sword; he believes in being prepared all the time and at every moment," Tukoji said. "Then he came to his room and hung up the sword."

"Around what time was it?"

"Late afternoon. Raje stored all his weapons, then he changed and left to have lunch with Aaisaheb, and yes, he asked me to tell you he specifically remembers running his hand over his beloved sword as usual, and thanking Aai Bhavani for her benevolence upon him and his people. He would have surely noted any missing jewels."

Prajakta moved forward to speak, then noticed the scorn on Tukoji's face. She blinked at his obvious dislike; was he one of those people who believed women should be quiet and subservient? It was hard to believe he hadn't learned from their King, who not only respected women but also took advice from Aaisaheb on so many matters of administration and policy. She kept her gaze focussed on the small dagger at his waist as she spoke, "Sir, we are not much aware of the current political news. Please can you tell us who you suspect of having a role to play in the theft?"

Tukoji sniffed, "You are just children, I don't see why… humph… alright, let's all sit here." He led them to the only window in the place, and they all squatted in the sunlight streaming in. "Our King has two principal enemies – Aurangzeb and Adil Shah. If we consider plots to stop the Coronation, these kingdoms have many men experienced enough to have done this. Then there are the English – after they revealed their true colours at Panhala, Raje refused to trust them and confiscated their precious cargo at Rajapur. Since then, they are subdued, but constantly trying to forge alliances against us." He stood up suddenly and stared out of the window. The children sat there on the floor, and waited for Tukoji to explain further.

The statesman leaned against the wall and sighed. "We are on good terms with the French; in fact, you could say they are our friends, but that may be only because they hate the English! They have their own agenda for coming all the way to our country, and it definitely isn't to improve our lives," he smiled.

Prajakta cleared her throat, but stayed silent.

"Do you have something more to ask?" Tukoji said wearily.

"What about our own people?" She raised her eyes to meet his. "Could one of them have done this?"

"What are you saying, Tai? As if our people would dare to touch the Bhavani!" Sarjya tugged at her hand, willing her to shut up.

"No, boy! She is right. We do have Sardars who side with the Mughals openly or in private, and they are a thorn in our side because they know the territory and don't immediately stand out as different amongst us," Tukoji said.

Ganya shuddered. "Enemies on all sides! This is a very dangerous place to be!"

"Yes, Ganya, but we have to eliminate all these people one by one. And remember, it could be someone totally unexpected too, like a person who just wanted the jewels to sell them for the money – nothing to do with politics at all!" Prajakta said.

Ganya slapped his forehead. "I am totally confused! This is like a game of chess – my cousin tried to explain it to me once, and I got a huge headache that lasted for three days and totally put me off food – I'll never forget that because it was Sankrant, and my mother had made a feast that day which I never got to eat!"

They all burst out laughing; even Tukoji's lips actually quivered.

"Sir, what would be the monetary value of the stolen gems, and where could a thief hope to sell them?" Sopan asked.

The statesman nodded his approval. "Good question! The stones are worth thousands of gold mohurs, but the emerald and ruby are large enough to arouse suspicion if someone tried to sell them. Raje has sent out indirect feelers to all the merchants around here, but no one has reported seeing such jewels."

"Or the person could just keep them hidden till the heat dies down!" Prajakta shook her head.

Tukoji glared at her before saying, "If the jewels are inside Raigad, we will find them!"

"They could have left the area long before the theft was noticed..." She became aware of his darkening face and stopped voicing her objections.

Sopan stepped forward, finally voicing what they all wanted, "Can we see the Bhavani Sword now?"

***

"Thank God Sopan asked to see the sword, Tukoji looked as if he wanted to throw you off Takmak Tok! By the way, when will we go to that place, Tai? Must be a wonderful view from there!" Sarjya whispered.

"I doubt the prisoners get to appreciate the scenery!" Prajakta made a face at him as they followed the others out of the room. She turned to take another glance at the weapons room just beyond the large bed, wondering how the thief had gotten away with the jewels in such a heavily guarded place.

"Tukoji is so resistant to the idea that we may actually be of any help," Sarjya said, "he gives each piece of information so reluctantly; it's almost as if he doesn't want the mystery to be solved!"

Chapter 13

Sarjya gripped Prajakta's hand tightly. They were finally going to be in the same room as the magnificent weapon! Tukoji led them out of the royal chambers, and down the hallway to a much smaller room. Two glaring guards also guarded this one; the low door had a massive iron lock on it. He took off a thread from around his neck and held up the two keys on it. "Only Raje and I have the keys." He opened the lock and, one by one, they bent low to enter the darkened room. Grabbing the torch from one of the guards, Tukoji held it aloft to gasps of astonishment from the Naikwadi children.

The flickering light reflected off the polished steel blades of the different weapons, lending the place a magical air. Sopan's hands itched to touch each one and admire the craftsmanship. He marvelled at the sheer range of weaponry – the swords, the *katyaar*s, the *dandpatta,* and even the *waghnakh* – the claw-like dagger that could be worn around the knuckles and concealed in one's palm. Perhaps this was the very one Raje used against Afzal Khan! He turned to Tukoji with a frown and asked, "Where are the three main swords?"

"We were very fortunate, son – at the time the thief entered the royal chambers to carry out his dastardly plot, the Jagdamba had just been sent for repairs; Raje had noticed a small nick in the blade. It is still with the swordsmith."

"And the Tulja?" Sarjya asked about the third famous sword of their King.

Tukoji had a baffled expression on his face. "The Tulja was on the rack, right next to the Bhavani Sword, but the thief appeared to have been interested only in the divine sword; he did not touch the Tulja." He moved to unlock an even smaller door that led into yet another room.

Sarjya pushed past him to peep into the smaller room. There, displayed on a rack, were the two swords. Sarjya's mouth hung open at the sight before him. *The Bhavani!* "Magnificent!" he whispered, his hands joined almost as if in prayer.

Sopan shuffled forward. "May I?" He moved into the inner room after a confirmation nod from Tukoji, and took down the scabbard first. The boy's trembling hands reverently lifted down the sword and bent for a closer look. He ran his fingers over the empty spaces on the hilt. "The edges are so rough," he exclaimed, "Raje's fingers would have got cut if he had run his fingers over this part."

"Yes," Tukoji's head bobbed as he spoke, "in fact, that was how our King detected the theft the next afternoon."

"So, Monday afternoon, the sword was confirmed to be intact, and on Tuesday afternoon, Raje cut his fingers on the rough edges. One whole day, afternoon to afternoon is what we have to focus on." Prajakta handed the list back to Tukoji.

"Don't you need to keep it?" he asked.

"Tai has a wonderful memory," Sarjya's voice rose, "she can tell you every name on the list!"

Tukoji's face brightened just the tiniest bit. Maybe there was hope after all – Aaisaheb was right, these children were definitely unusual!

They returned to the royal chambers to find Rama waiting for them outside the main door. "Aaisaheb has sent me to help you today." She looked at Tukoji and said, "Sir, you are needed in the new hall – some issue with the pillars being uneven."

The statesman patted the thread around his neck, as if to make sure the two keys were there. He looked into the King's rooms and then at Rama. "Make sure everything is as it was and lock the place up tighter than… humph… well, tight!" His high-pitched voice belied the stern words as he turned and walked out.

"Phew!" Sarjya said and dropped to squat on the floor outside the weapon's room. "What a surly man!"

"He has so much responsibility," Rama said, "and he's taken this theft very hard, especially now that nearly five days have passed and he hasn't found even a clue."

"We found one, Rama Tai!" Sarjya jumped up again.

"Really? What clever children you are!" she said, beaming. "*Chala*, now tell me what else you need to know. Let's all sit down for a while."

Prajakta gathered Kaloo up in her arms and began to arrange the facts as they now knew them. "Raje came to his room after his rounds on Monday and hung up his sword."

"Which was intact," Sopan added.

"Yes," Prajakta said, "then he went to eat with Aaisaheb."

"Did anyone help him change or come to take away his clothes?" Ganya asked.

"Very good, Ganya. You are right, we should know that." Prajakta patted his back.

They all turned to Rama, even Kaloo tilted his head in enquiry.

"Hmm," Rama thought for a while before answering, "Soyarabaisaheb usually greets him when he returns from outside, and accompanies him for lunch, but that day she had been called away as Shambhu Raje was feverish; she was by his side till late at night."

Prajakta asked, "What had happened to him? Did he have chills or any yellow tinge to his eyes?"

"I'm not sure, I think he had agonizing stomach pain too."

Sarjya groaned, "Tai, the Prince has an expert *vaidya* to think of all that. We are here for something else!" He turned to Rama and continued, "So Raje was by himself till he left for food?"

Rama said, "Yes, but..." Her eyes widened. "Her maid, Chandra, had come to give Raje the message that her mistress could not be there that day."

"Does she wear mogras in her hair?" Sopan asked.

Rama touched her own bun. "We all do at festivals, but I've never noticed her wearing flowers at other times. Besides, I'm sure she gave the message to the guards, or then to Raje at the very entrance. You mentioned the flower was found in the innermost room, the dressing area, right? She could never have been in there."

"*Chhya,* one possibility gone!" Sarjya groaned and flopped dramatically onto the stone floor. "I am tired!"

"Already?" Prajakta glared at him. "It's barely been an hour since you woke up."

"But I didn't sleep *na,* Tai; you woke me up so early. Besides, it's so nice and cool in this corner, away from sunlight – no wonder the King's bed is positioned here. Ow!"

Prajakta cuffed him and then ruffled his hair. "You are Sarjya Naik, not Sarjerao Bhosale – sit up and pay attention!" She sobered and looked at the beautiful woman. "Rama Tai, what happened after Chandra gave the message to Raje?"

"Then Raje went alone for lunch with Aaisaheb. He came back after food and lay down for an hour. Just before dark, his clothier visited."

"What's that?" Sopan asked.

"Who's that, you mean! He's the person who stitches clothes for the King," Rama said.

"*Oho,* tailor!" Sarjya guffawed. "Royal people give royal names for their staff!" He pulled Kaloo's ears, making the dog jump. "I wonder what royal dogs are called? Kaloo could be Sawlerao!"

"How many years has he – this tailor – been with our King?" Prajakta asked after the merriment at his words had died down.

Rama leaned back against the wall and ran her fingers lovingly over the blue satin bedspread. "Raje's tailor is Ganpat Shinde."

Ganya looked up interestedly. Another Ganpat!

"He's been our King's personal tailor for the last five years; he came here from Indore." Rama paused as if she was wondering how best to frame her next words. "You may find his appearance a little strange. His nose is unusually long, so the people who found him called him Ganpat, after the elephant God. He was abandoned by his parents and found by a tribe of gypsies who raised him. One day, he grew tired of their nomadic existence and decided to stay in Indore; he apprenticed with a tailor named Shinde. The man worked exclusively for the Royal Family of Indore, and was famous for his lavish embroidery, especially with pearls. Ganpat adopted his mentor's surname and became like a son to him. As his skills grew, so did his reputation, and soon he began to be wooed by princely families across the country. Our Aaisaheb offered him his own house and workshop in Pune, and won him over."

Rama's eyes filled with tears. "He had a pretty wife and a son, Shubham," she sniffed and explained. "Ganpat's wife was a devotee of Aai Bhavani, and believed our Raje was an avatar of God. Her deepest desire was that her son should be in Raje's army. Shubham was a tall, strapping man, good-looking and always smiling – the apple of his father's eye! Ganpat was so proud of him that he would boast about him at every opportunity. And then…," Rama wiped her tears and sighed. "Then Salher happened."

The children's faces fell in unison at the mention of the great battle, where so much was won, but so much was lost as well.

Rama continued softly, "Shubham was killed in battle. Ganpat's wife refused to believe her son was dead; she kept waiting for him to return. Every day she'd set out three plates for their meals… then it slowly began to dawn on her that her precious son was never coming back. She refused to eat and began to wither before our very eyes. Aaisaheb even visited their home to speak to her, but the woman just faded away. Ganpat was inconsolable." Rama wiped her cheeks before continuing, "Now he lives in the fort itself and keeps trying to convince Raje to take him into battle with him. He practices sword fighting in his spare time, though he risks injuring his fingers and jeopardizing his job; he has vowed to kill as many Mughals as he can and avenge his family." The children had to strain to hear Rama's next words, "Poor man! Some people have given everything to the cause."

They sat there in silence for a while, then became aware of the soft snores emanating from Sarjya. Prajakta blushed; her brother was beginning to embarrass them in front of everyone! She pinched his arm, and his eyes flew open.

"What did you do that for?" he asked, bleary-eyed. "If I can't sleep in the King's bed, at least let me enjoy dreaming on the floor next to it. Why did you disturb me? Have you solved the mystery already?"

Prajakta had just raised her hand to smack him when he pointed to the wall next to his head and yelled, "Wait a minute, did you see that?"

They all turned to where Sarjya was pointing; there was a small, lighter patch on the stone wall. He got up and bent for a closer look.

Prajakta and Rama peeped over his shoulder, but the area was deep in shadow, and even in broad daylight they needed more illumination for a clearer view. Rama asked the guards to light a torch and hurried over to hold the flame over the area. Sopan ran his fingers over the patch, remarking, "It's just a rough area between two stones. I need... I need to just..." He fiddled around some more and drew up with a gasp. "There's something here! A space, just a small one!" He straightened and said, "but it's empty."

"Are you sure? Let me see!" Sarjya pushed Sopan aside, but he couldn't feel anything inside either. Prajakta looked down at the floor below; there were no broken pieces of the wall. "Rama Tai," she turned to the puzzled woman and said, "did the sweeper mention finding any debris here on the day of the theft?"

"I'll ask him," Ramas's eyes gleamed. This was definitely a big clue. "Raje's room was being spruced up as part of the preparations; in fact, it had been resurfaced just a fortnight ago. There was no way the gap could have been there after that!" She darted out to contact Tukoji.

"Woof woof!" The startled children looked to their right. But Kaloo was in Sarjya's arms, and he was to their left, so now where was the... oh, it was Ganya! They all burst out laughing. "You are getting better and better at imitation, Ganya! It's wonderful to hear your amazing mimicry again."

The Queen Mother's entry abruptly silenced their merriment. "*Arre wah,* children, you have already created quite a disturbance in our palace!"

"Sorry, Aaisaheb," Prajakta began.

"No, no, lass; I meant all the clues you have been picking up. Shivba's men were more focussed on the suspects; no one paid so much attention to the room, thinking it was of no use now that the jewels had already gone."

Chapter 14

"Er, Aaisaheb?" Sopan ventured.

"Yes, child?" The Queen Mother perched at the edge of the bed and smiled at him.

"After the meeting of ministers on Monday night, did Raje leave his chambers again, and did anyone else enter?"

"Also…," Prajakta tugged her plait and asked, "what exact symptoms did Sambhaji Raji have?"

"Bal Sambhaji?" The regal monarch frowned. "What's that got to do with?" She looked up as Tukoji re-entered with Rama. He bowed to the Queen Mother and moved to check out the crevice they had discovered, almost shoving Sarjya aside.

"Hmm," he said, "it's definitely recent, but the area has been swept in the morning, and no one reported any breakage. I've summoned Hari, the sweeper, but I think it'll turn out to be nothing – maybe an indication that the masons did a shoddy job."

"Or not!" Sarjya whispered loudly and looked away, refusing to meet Tukoji's eyes.

Shivaji's aide walked through the rooms, checking every nook and cranny, but that was the only unusual gap he found in the rocks. He scratched his head, muttering to himself, then he measured the height of the crevice from the ground and looked under the adjacent bed. "Hmm," he said again.

"Saheb, you called?" The emaciated man who entered noticed the Queen Mother and backed away. "Sorry, sorry, Aaisaheb, I didn't see you!" He bowed low and stayed that way as if frozen.

The Queen Mother looked at Tukoji and gestured for him to speak to the man.

"Hari," Tukoji said, tugging the bewildered man's arm impatiently. "Look here, look!" He pointed to the floor beneath the crevice. "Was there any debris here on Tuesday morning?"

The man gave Tukoji a blank look.

"Hari, four days ago, were there any small pieces of stone on the floor in that area?" Aaisaheb spoke gently and patiently.

"No, Aaisaheb." The man bowed once more, his right hand shaking as he raised it to tug at his lips. Everyone in the room groaned; they had thought they were onto something good. "But," Hari continued, "it was there two days ago."

Two days ago!

They all wore matching expressions of incredulity.

"So, it crumbled two days ago?" With a sigh, Sarjya said, "Then it's of no use to us."

"I knew you kids were not needed here!" Tukoji was almost jubilant.

"What? What did you say?" Sarjya had his arms akimbo.

"Nothing." The man's stony expression spoke volumes. "I never said anything to you. *Chala* Aaisaheb, I don't think your precious time needs to be wasted here anymore." He ushered the Queen Mother outside. The children heard him mutter 'childish clues', and 'wandering about' before exiting.

Hari stood there, scratching his head and muttering to himself,

"I swear I saw such gravel last week also, but…" He gave Prajakta a toothless smile and mumbled, "I must be getting old, my eyesight is not what it used to be. Maybe Tukoji will fire me also, along with the mason who worked on the wall!"

"Did you hear him, Tai?" Sarjya was almost spitting with fury at Tukoji's words.

"Yes, Sarjya," Prajakta put her hand on his shoulder and said, "yes, we all heard him! Calm down."

"I… I will…," he choked, and stomped out of the room.

Ganya looked at Prajakta and Sopan, then ran after his best friend, closely followed by Kaloo. Prajakta gave the crevice one last puzzled look, before walking out with Sopan. "We need to ask about what exactly happened in the meeting, and the next day, before Raje discovered the theft." She tugged her right plait. "Why would the debris in only that room keep falling? Every other place in the fort seems sturdy enough to last for centuries."

Sopan also turned back to glance at the disturbed area with a frown. Surely the royal chambers didn't have mice that burrowed into walls!

They were halfway down the steps when they ran into Ganya and Kaloo.

"*Arre,* where did Sarjya go?" Ganya asked.

"Why are you asking us? Didn't you just go after him?"

"We did, but he… he suddenly vanished! Even Kaloo couldn't find him; he ran up and down the steps a few times, then led me here," Ganya replied.

Prajakta slapped her forehead. "I hope he's not doing something silly; as it is, everyone is on edge after the theft, and we are outsiders here. Only a few people know us."

"You mean to say they might think Sarjya is the thief?" Ganya was flabbergasted.

"Anything is possible." Prajakta muttered. Her worried face upset Kaloo, who began to howl. "Shh, shh, Kaloo, it's ok, we'll find him, but first let's go to our room; he may have already gone there to pout."

"Or sleep!" Sopan said and smiled.

"Afterwards, we can ask for something to eat!" Ganya said shyly, "I don't know why, but my appetite has returned all of a sudden."

"Must be because now you are surrounded by colours and pomp and show!" Prajakta beamed. "That's your favourite ambience, right, Sopan? Sopan?" She turned to find him frowning at his fingers. "What is it?"

"I don't know how I got hurt; my fingers are bleeding," Sopan said. "Must be a sharp edge on one of the stones. What were you saying, Tai? Aah, yes, Ganya becomes pale and listless in bland surroundings – absolutely correct. Ganya, you need drama and larger-than-life things around you; no wonder Sarjya is your best friend!"

The children burst into their rooms, hoping to find Sarjya there, but it was empty except for Rama. "There you are! Come," she said, "Aaisaheb told me to give you an early lunch."

"But we need to ask Tukoji more questions!" Prajakta said.

"Rama Tai, are there many mice in the fort?" Sopan asked almost simultaneously.

Rama chortled. "What strange things you children think of! That man is having a tough time as it is; he hates all kids, even his own. And Sopan – we have a plump, arrogant tabby cat called Jilbya because of his colour, and the way he winds around our legs and trips us up all the time. How come you haven't seen him yet?" Her eyes lit up at her next words, "Of course, your Kaloo must have scared him off. I'll keep an eye out for him. Come, let's eat first. Where's-"

"Tai!" Sarjya screeched to a halt at the sight of the beautiful woman. "Rama Tai!" he amended.

"*Chala, chala,* growing children need to eat," Rama ordered them to the dining hall, past the workers staggering under heavy loads of chikoos and bananas.

Prajakta gave Sarjya a questioning glance; he looked sideways at Rama and lifted his chin, indicating they should talk later.

Prajakta gulped down her food as fast as she could, aware of Sarjya's imploring gaze on hers. Rama continued to talk, "How are your parents? Is it very hot in Naikwadi?" She seemed to have endless questions.

"Enough," Sarjya said and stood up. "We're done!"

"But… but," Ganya looked down at his half-eaten plate and sputtered, "I'm still…," he stopped at the look on Sarjya's face and bent to pick up four of the seven pedhas on his plate. He hurriedly stuffed them into the pockets of his kurta and shovelled the rest into his mouth.

"Umphh, wumph!" he tried to protest with a full mouth as Sarjya dragged him back to their room.

Prajakta smiled at Rama. "Rama Tai, we'll just come back in a little while; Ganya needs to change his clothes, please wait here for us."

In their room, Sopan thumped a red-faced Ganya on the back while Prajakta brought him some water to drink.

"Why did you swallow so much at once?" Sarjya chastised him.

"Why did you make me get up so soon then?" he retorted.

"Ok, ok, quit fighting you two. Rama Tai is waiting for us. Sarjya, quickly tell us where you went and what you learned."

"Tai, I was so mad at that Tukoji," Sarjya said, clenching his fists, "I just wanted to smash something. I went in the opposite direction from him and got lost in all those corridors and staircases. I found myself in a shadowy hallway with only one flickering torch at the end. Suddenly, there was a strange shuffling sound, and then a woman laughed."

"*Baapre*!" Ganya had recovered enough to speak clearly. "Was she a *chandain*?"

"Shut up, Ganya, there is no such thing as ghosts!" Prajakta gave him an exasperated look, then turned to her brother to enquire, "Then what happened?"

Sarjya beamed at his friends' eager faces. "Just then, a deep and dangerous voice whispered in Hindi, 'you did well *meri jaan*, here's the pair of silver anklets I promised you!' Then there was a tinkling sound, and then the man said, 'How long does the effect of the poison last?'"

"Poison!" Prajakta's jaw dropped.

"The woman replied, 'Two days. I gave him a small dose only; people would get suspicious.' '*Shabbash meri Rani*,' the man replied, and the pair laughed before abruptly falling silent. I tried to move closer, but a guard called out to another from somewhere beyond, and the two scurried off even further, and vanished into one of the passages before I could make out which one. It took me ages, stumbling into different rooms and halls, till I finally found my way back to our room. This place is like a maze!" Sarjya turned expectantly to his sister and asked, "What did you make of the conversation, Tai? Do you think it could be connected to the theft?"

She tapped her lips. "I…"

"*Arre*, children, what are you all doing here, and why hasn't Ganya changed yet?" Rama frowned at them.

"He was feeling a little giddy, Rama Tai," Sarjya pushed Ganya down to the floor. "We decided to wait here for a little while. Tsk tsk, all that food!" he shook his head. "That's why his kurta burst!"

Ganya's eyes widened; he turned his face to the other side to avoid glaring at Sarjya.

"Poor thing!" Rama giggled. "Take rest. Let's sit here only till he feels better. Do you want me to call the *healer*?"

"No, no," Prajakta was quick to answer, "I gave him some fennel, he'll feel better soon. Now, Rama Tai, let's talk about the day after the theft. What was Raje's schedule? Who all entered his chambers?"

Chapter 15

"Aaisaheb?"

The Queen Mother turned around from the window she was gazing out of, her face creasing into smiles at the sight of her beloved son. Shivaji stooped to take her blessings, then led her to the comfortable divan. She watched as he ran his fingers over the dark velvet cloth. "Shivba, you are uncharacteristically silent. What troubles you today, my child?" she asked.

The King's earrings bobbed as he shook his head ruefully and said, "I never could hide anything from you, mother! My spies have brought news that the Adil Shahi House is furious that the Coronation is taking place. I still think-"

The Queen Mother interrupted, "We must follow Pandit Gagabhatt's advice; we need this Coronation for our Kingdom to be recognized formally."

Shivaji sighed. "Yes, Mother, I accept his wisdom even though you know I am not one for such a show of extravagance. It's just that we are surrounded by enemies – both obvious and hidden – and you know, after Kondaji Farzand's heroics in winning Panhala for us, Sikander Adil Shah's advisers in his government remain determined to take revenge.

They are constantly wary of us allying with Aurangzeb and posing an even bigger threat. And now this grand ceremony will risk aggravating them all. My man inside the Adil Shahi administration has warned of a plot targeting the Coronation; he said there were rumblings of a direct attack, but perhaps this theft of jewels was part of a scheme to unsettle us."

The Queen Mother considered his words, her stern expression indicating what she thought of the Bijapur Kingdom that had cost her not only her marriage but also a son. She said, softly, "It is a common belief that the Bhavani Sword empowers you in all your battles. Our people's faith in Aai Bhavani is of immeasurable support to us all, so striking at the sword would be just the kind of plot those treacherous people could hatch. That is exactly why we have kept news about the missing jewels a secret, so that our people don't panic."

Shivaji nodded. "So, do you think the theft was the whole plan, or just the first move of their strategy? Should we replace the precious stones and continue as before?"

"Yes, we need to carry on. Your men and," with a smile, the Queen Mother added, "my special soldiers will find out who is responsible, and then we can predict the next few steps."

Raje took her wrinkled hand into his. "Soyara tells me Sambhaji's better now and should be totally fine within a couple of days."

The Queen Mother toyed with the pearls around her neck. "Something is worrying me, Shivba; we need to be careful about our health. Our enemies are all around and …"

"Don't worry, Aaisaheb, this was just a little thing; Shambhu probably swallowed too much river water or ate something gone bad. It happens to everyone; don't let small things disturb you."

"I wish Sai were still with us!" A tear ran down the Queen Mother's face at the memory of Sambhaji's mother.

Shivaji held her hand a little tighter and gave her a tender smile. "I do too."

The sound of a throat being cleared came from the doorway, and Moropant entered after the Queen Mother and King indicated he could come in. "Raje," he said, "an English captain from Mumbra, was heard a few days ago boasting of a plan to create problems in the Coronation. He said, 'Our King will rule over you all; no one else can call himself King here – we will make sure of that!'" Moropant added, "All the firangis were very drunk at that time, so our spies didn't think it very important, but passed on the news to us just the same."

"Those *goras*!" Shivaji muttered angrily, his cowrie necklace clinking as he stood up, "always meddling in our affairs! Why don't they go back to their own country? They don't have the guts to attack us directly, always finding enemies of ours to befriend."

"They are already seething over the Surat raids, and now they are worried we will lean towards the French. They are just the sort to covet the jewels – I've heard they like to acquire such things of cultural value from different countries." Jeejabai remarked, her eyes burning with fury. "Who knows, maybe they wanted to steal the sword itself, but had to make do with some jewels! After all, without the distinctive Bhavani at your side under the royal umbrella, no one could visualize this Coronation being quite complete."

The three statesmen became thoughtful. Who could have hatched this deceitful plan? Moropant's earrings danced, his head moving in tune with his thoughts. "It pains me to say this, but one of our own could be involved in the plan. We need to doubt everyone and double-check all information."

"Let's not get paranoid yet. I have faith in our investigators; they're taking it slow and steady," Raje said, "let's figure out how the theft took place first, and who was the immediate thief. We can then get an idea about the puppeteer behind the players. Mother," he smiled at Aaisaheband asked, "how are our little sleuths faring so far?"

"They've already unearthed some unusual things and irritated Tukoji," she said with a chuckle.

Moropant's cheeks dimpled. "It doesn't take much to upset that man! In fact, it seems that one of the children is a great mimic and imitates Tukoji so well that even Rama was taken in. I hope our Tukoji never hears of it; he already was sputtering when I told him to grant the children full access to all parts of the fort!"

***

"You're unusually quiet." Prajakta nudged her brother.

He spat out the piece of fingernail he was chewing on and looked down at his hand and the missing fingertip. Should he voice his fears, or was he dramatizing the situation as usual? Sarjya looked into Prajakta's worried eyes and decided to speak up. "I know who the villain is!"

The duo turned at the loud gasp from behind them. Ganya's mouth was hanging open at the news. "Tell me, tell me who it is? How do you know? Did you see someone with the jewels? I knew you would solve this mystery first, my friend!"

"Who solved what?" Sopan slapped Sarjya on his back and asked, "What are you all talking about?"

"Sarjya knows who the thief is!" Ganya beamed.

Three questioning faces turned to Sarjya, who flushed. "I mean… I think… I…," he sat straighter and blurted out, "It's Tukoji!"

The stunned silence that followed his words elicited a gratified smile from Sarjya, who rushed to explain. "He's been against us from the moment we came here; he protests every time Aaisaheb trusts us or tells us privileged news. He's always hanging around our rooms asking us what we're doing. He hates Kaloo, too! I think he knows we will expose him, and so he wants us gone."

Sopan rubbed his forehead and said, "Did you ever notice he carries a dagger in his cummerbund? An aide doing administrative work… why would he need a weapon? I agree with Sarjya, there's something fishy there!"

Prajakta tugged her plaits. "We need better reasons to suspect him. I'm not saying you're wrong… he's in a great position to easily steal the stones, and he's always nervous around us… but we need proof before we can tell Aaisaheb of our suspicions."

"I will follow him tonight!" Sarjya said.

"Me too!" Ganya stood up.

"I… I don't think you should go alone, Sarjya, but we all can't go with you – it'll be too noisy. You are the stealthy one." Prajakta said, looking to Sopan for help.

He nodded. "I'll find out where Tukoji's quarters are. We'll fix a time and a route. I'll be a few yards behind Sajya in case he needs help."

Sarjya bristled at the thought of assistance, but the sombre look on Prajakta's face told him it wasn't negotiable.

"We'll continue to ask questions and consider other possibilities too, till we are sure Sarjya's suspicions are correct," Prajakta said.

***

The cool evening breeze blew a few strands of hair onto Rama's face as she watched the children savour their meal; she felt a pang of regret at not kissing her little girl goodbye. The child would always cling to her, and mother and daughter would both end up in tears, so of late, Rama had been leaving while her girl was still sleeping. There was so much extra work Aaisaheb needed help with, and only a week left before the grand ceremony. She sighed to herself. Maybe after the guests had all returned, she'd have time for her little *chakuli.*

"Rama Tai?" Prajakta had eaten and washed her hands during Rama's ruminations. She wiped her hands on her skirt and said, "Please give me the list of people who entered Raje's chambers the day after the council meeting, that is Tuesday."

So focussed this girl is, Rama marvelled. *I want my daughter to be just like her!* She said, "Raje got up at the crack of dawn, dressed and left for the temple. Hari cleaned the room, then Raje returned a couple of hours later to supervise the preparations in the new hall. Soyara Baisaheb then came with her maid to keep some washed clothes and change the sheets."

"Which maid? What was her name?" Prajakta asked.

"Chandra."

"The same one who gave Raje the message the previous day?"

"Yes."

"Hmm," Prajakta pursed her lips and asked, "this Chandra, how old is she? What does she look like? Where is she from? Is she married?"

Rama's eyes narrowed; why was Prajakta asking about the maid? Did she think.... surely not! Aloud, she said, "Chandra is around 24-25. She's unmarried – she says the love of her life died in the Battle of Salher, and she will never marry now."

"So, she is from this area and stays within the fort? And her surname?" Prajakta persisted with her questions.

"She...," Rama thought for a while before speaking, "I think she is from Nashik, but actually she never speaks much of her people, only of her beloved who died. I never asked her surname, actually...she doesn't wear *kunkoo,* but that's-" she tapered off, doubt now clearly visible on her face. Her green glass bangles clinked as she scratched her head and said, "But she does speak Hindi surprisingly well, perhaps she had some neighbours or friends who conversed in Hindi."

"And you've never seen flowers in her hair?" Sarjya asked.

Again with the flowers! Rama groaned. "That Hari must have dragged in something from outside when he cleaned. How would any ordinary woman enter Raje's dressing room? And Soyarabaisaheb hates the smell of mogras, so even her maids are forbidden from wearing those flowers – it sets her off into bouts of sneezing!"

Prajakta nodded, then asked, "Is it... is it possible we can talk to Rani Soyara?"

"I will ask her, I'm sure she will make some time for you now that Shambhu Raje is feeling better." Rama gave a dazed smile; did the girl suspect the Queen, too?

Sopan now took up the questions. "So, we were talking about the day the theft was discovered – after the Queen and her maid left, no one came in?"

"No," said Rama. "Raje returned after lunch to change for a meeting, and he happened to observe that the sword was not in its usual place, but on the rack belonging to the Jagdamba. He was puzzled by the displacement, but when he lifted the sword to put it back in its usual place, he realized the jewels were missing, as was the scabbard. He immediately sent for Tukoji and Moropant, and gave orders to search every man, woman and child before they exited the fort."

"But he didn't mention this to anyone else, except Aaisaheb?" Sopan confirmed.

"No."

"Not even the Queen?"

Rama had no answer.

"*Accha*!" Sarjya puffed up his cheeks and then blew out air loudly., "Rama Tai, how many men regularly guard Raje's chambers?" he asked.

"There are two guards at the door, and two each at either end of the hallway, so six in total at a time. Their duty changes every eight hours, and there are three such groups, so a total of 18 men have been entrusted with this important task," Rama said.

Kaloo began to squirm, so Sarjya got up to take him out. "All talk and no action has gotten him bored. Rama Tai, can we go to the *Hatti Talav* and watch the elephants bathing?"

Ganya's eyes lit up. Elephants! One more animal sound he needed to work on. He scrambled to his feet. "I also want to go!"

Prajakta and Sopan looked at each other; this plan held appeal for them too, but the combination of excited boys, a mischievous dog, and gigantic elephants was a scary one. Prajakta looked to the heavens and prayed her impulsive brother didn't try to ride Raje's elephant – after all, he had already tried to copy their King in so many more dangerous ways. She waggled a finger at him, hoping he understood he was to stay out of mischief. But Sarjya only rolled his eyes and stepped out, just managing to avoid bumping into the soldier who was entering.

The soldier called Rama aside, and the two spoke for a few minutes. Then, she rushed back to the children, simmering with excitement. "Tukoji has sent a message. He said all of the guards had been interrogated before, and their quarters were searched, but after today's discovery of the disturbed masonry and the mogra flower, they were questioned again. They are mostly simple folks dedicated to their King."

"Mostly?" Prajakta caught the word.

Rama gave a sheepish smile. "One of them, Mukund Gujar, an unmarried man from Sholapur – he likes to visit uhm," Rama said, her cheeks tinged with crimson, "uhm, uhm, dancing women. During this raid, he was found to have an unusually large amount of money hidden under his pile of clothes and… a *gajra* of mogra flowers!"

Chapter 16

Mukund Gujar sat with his head held in his hands. The grey-haired guard looked at him pityingly through the bars; even he knew this man was in deep trouble. Sweat dripped down Gujar's brow and into his palms. *Why had he been so stupid? Was this why his old parents had sent him here from Mahad*? 'Serve your King, make us proud.' his father had said, blessing him with trembling hands. 'Our village is only full of old people now; all the men have gone off to fight for Swarajya. There is nothing for you here.'

'But Baba,' he had protested with a glance at his blind mother, 'who will look after you and Aai?'

She raised her unseeing gaze at his words and said, '*Arre bala*, don't worry about me. I'm blessed to have a son like you – *Shravan bal ahes tu*! You are taking such good care of us. But we mustn't be selfish, now your King needs you too. One day, our country will remember your name, my son!'

Gujar thought of the bright-eyed, dedicated soldier he had been at first – how he had stood ramrod straight on his first posting outside the gate to Raigad Fort, quivering with pride, hungry only for a look of approval from his Subhedar. A few months in, he had grown fond of drink and watching tamashas. He began to lean against the wall while on duty, even caught a few winks when no one was looking, desperately counting down the hours till his shift ended. Then, he had stopped sending home money and squandered all his earnings on his new hobbies. Gujar groaned and slapped his forehead. "What have I done!"

Rama put up her hands to quell the children's outburst of questions about the imprisoned guard. "Wait, wait! Ask me one by one," she told them.

"Who gave him the money?" Sarjya asked. He and Ganya had delayed their exit to the Talav to listen to the guard's message. They could watch the elephants another time – things were simply more interesting here! In the pause before Rama's answer, they could hear the clattering of horses' hooves and orders being shouted as a small troop of soldiers arrived. Sarjya grinned. It sounded like things were heating up!

"It seems Gujar had won that money gambling," Rama said.

"So, it wasn't a bribe from the thief, perhaps someone who was rich and in a high position?" Sarjya was crestfallen.

"No," Rama frowned at his disgusted expression before continuing, "but he did admit to allowing one of the dancing girls into Raje's rooms!"

"How come no one noticed this?" Sopan was quick to ask. "Aren't there two guards at a time outside the main door?"

Rama nodded. "Apparently, two of the dancing girls appeared together – one pretended to fall so the guards rushed to help her while Gujar smuggled the other, his girlfriend, in for just a moment to show her Raje's chambers quickly."

"When did this happen?" Prajakta asked.

"On Monday morning, the day before the theft was discovered."

"So, it has nothing to do with the missing jewels." Prajakta's face fell.

Ganya added, "Because Raje is sure the sword was intact till Monday afternoon!"

"*Chhya*!" Sarjya tossed a pebble at the wall, and an excited Kaloo ran to fetch it.

"That means Gujar is in trouble, but not for the theft...wait a minute," Prajakta said, "did the girl go into the royal dressing room? Was she wearing mogra flowers in her hair?"

Rama smiled and said, "Yes, Gujar confirmed that she wanted to take a quick peek at the King's necklaces and rings. He insists she saw them from afar, and he was holding on to her arm tightly to stop her touching anything. So, the flower must have fallen then and been kicked behind the cupboard later, mystery solved!"

Sarjya slapped his forehead and groaned. "Now Tukoji will again say, 'all you children found are useless things that have no connection with the theft!'"

"I knew you had no place here; go back to your tiny little village today itself!"

Rama and the children turned their angry faces to the doorway, ready to face Tukoji, but there was no one there. Sarjya let out a roar of laughter and yelled, "Ganya, you got us good this time!"

Amidst the merriment and hooting, they heard the same voice again. "There you are!"

"*Kay re* Ganya, you can't fool us again with that girlish voice; at least wait a whi…," Prajakta's words died at the sight of Tukoji standing there.

The big man spoke in his thin voice, "Our men have found a copy of the Bhavani Sword buried in the soil a little way away from the *Maha Darwaza*. We're checking it out – just thought you should know – that is, if you have time." The man turned and scurried away.

"Did he hear me?" A worried Ganya clutched Prajakta's arm.

She shook her head. "I don't think so, but…,"

"Oh God, as it is, he hates us! Now he will be even more unpleasant." Sarjya groaned. "But what was he saying about the sword?"

They all got up to follow, but Tukoji had vanished into the fort.

"Let's go after him!" Sarjya stood up and looked at Rama. "Please! Where did he go?"

"I wouldn't know!" Rama said.

"The royal chambers – it has to be! Rama Tai, take us there." he begged.

"Shut up, Sarjya!" Prajakta pulled him away from Rama. "Let Raje and his men handle that. Besides, if Tukoji really heard Ganya, it would be wiser to keep our distance for a while and hope he cools down!"

"But who buried a sword there? What did he mean by copy? Is the sword another magical blessing by Goddess Bhavani?" Sarjya almost cried with frustration. "He didn't say!"

"We can't go after Tukoji," Rama said; then, looking at the downcast faces, she spoke again, "but we can go to the Maha Darwaza and try to understand what happened."

***

The imposing Maha Darwaza was built at the entrance to Raigad Fort and was shut at sunset every day. The gigantic wooden door had iron spikes studded along its length to deter enemy elephants, and the towering bastions on either side were nearly 70 feet high. The steep pathway leading up to the door was the only way inside the fort. Two days ago, when the children arrived, it was almost midnight, and they had only a few seconds to appreciate the beautiful lotus carvings before the door was opened to let them in. Now, they all stopped to gape at the enormous structure, and then walked a few steps down the slope to the breathtaking view into the valley on all sides.

"There!" Sarjya pointed to a group of men gathered about two furlongs below. He scrambled downhill, half-running, half-falling, fully deaf to the desperate pleas of Prajakta and Rama to be more careful.

Alerted by the cries of the females, the men looked up and quickly stepped aside to avoid being carried downhill by the now frantically sliding boy. In the nick of time, a muscular fellow shot out a hand and grabbed Sarjya's collar, arresting what could have been a very long fall.

"Phew!" Sarjya smiled at the now stern man.

"What in the blazes were you trying to do? Commit suicide?" he asked.

"Why would I want to die? I'm only a child! And who are you?" Sarjya yelled back at him. "I was just coming to join you all."

"Join us all?" The burly man let out a loud bellow of laughter. "You sure are a funny boy!"

"I'm Sarjya Naik from Naikwadi," Sarjya said proudly.

"Naikwadi?" another man stepped up to ask. "That's far away. What are you doing here?"

What do these people know about our royal friends? We're part of the inner circle! Sarjya's chest puffed with pride, and he said, "Aaisaheb has called us…"

"We've come to put together a small performance for the Coronation," Sopan's gasping breaths punctuated his words; he had raced downhill, unable to stop his friend's fall, but just in time to prevent him from putting his foot in his mouth. Again.

Sarjya was sure all that running had addled Sopan's brains. "What perfo-" but Sopan put his arms around him and squeezed hard. "Secret, remember?" he whispered.

"Ah! Yes, yes, we are here for…. what he said."

"But Kaka, what are all of you looking at?" Sopan tried to divert any further questions.

"Last week, a team of Englishmen came to the fort with a translator." The burly man continued to glare at the squirming Sarjya as if he suspected the boy of the worst kind of mischief. "I was also on duty that day. They brought gifts for Raje and Aaisaheb. Raje had just left for a meeting with the village headmen of a few villages below – in fact, I was surprised they didn't meet the riders on their way up. When we told the Englishmen that no one could meet the Royal Family that day, the group was taken aback. They had a lengthy discussion among themselves before deciding to turn back. On the way down, one of them threw something into the valley; it looked like a bundle wrapped in a cloth. We shouted to alert them, but the translator yelled back that it was just leftover food. Some of us tried to look for the package, but we couldn't see anything in the bushes from above, so we left it at that. This morning, at sunrise, I saw light reflecting off a shiny object down there – a rat must have gnawed on the gunny bag to reveal the metallic contents."

Sarjya looked down to where the man was pointing and gulped; it was a long, steep fall from where he was standing. Rubbing his thumb on the remnant of his little finger, he wondered when he would learn to think before acting.

"*Wah*, you sure are observant, Kaka!" Sopan said to the now chuffed man, who then began to explain how they had tied ropes and made their way down the dangerous decline to investigate the contents of the bundle.

"But why would they throw the sword there?" Sarjya blurted out, then covered his mouth.

Sopan rushed to explain, "We overheard some people in the fort saying something about finding a sword, so we came here to find out for ourselves."

The man nodded, still distrustful of Sarjya, but refused to part with any more information. He turned his back to them with a gruff, "This is important official business, no children allowed here. Go back inside!"

Sopan dragged his grumbling friend back up the slope. saying, "Sarjya, if you want to be a good spy, you have to learn to be quiet when someone is already giving you information. You should have." An irate Prajakta drowned out his next words.

"You silly boy! Why do you rush off headfirst into every situation?" she screamed. "You could have been killed!"

"What rubbish! I would not!" Sarjya looked at the unshed tears in his sister's eyes and decided not to say anything else. Rama escorted the uncharacteristically silent group back to their room and left to inform the Queen Mother of the latest news.

"Tai, please speak to me," Sarjya beseeched his sister.

Prajakta screwed her eyes shut and shook her head, her plaits flying around her face. "This time, you have gone too far, Sarjya! This foolhardy behaviour has got to stop. You have been kidnapped, broken your leg, lost half a finger, and then nearly fallen into a ravine today. And you want to follow Tukoji around at night, too. You're only a child...I can't... I just can't!" She burst into tears.

The shocked boys looked at each other, not sure what to do. Kaloo crawled to Prajatka and whined. Sopan looked at the sobbing girl and signalled to Sarjya and Ganya to come out of the room with him. "Just let her calm down," he told them. "Come, let's sit there," he pointed to a small stone bench in the courtyard, away from the workers carting limestone, bundles of cloth and huge pots of water.

Ganya wrung his fingers and whispered, "I've never seen Tai so angry!"

Sarjya hung his head; he hadn't told his friends exactly what had happened in Sangamner.

A wave of excitement spread through the courtyard.

Shivaji Raje ale!

Shivaji Raje ale!

The boys hurriedly got to their feet as their King walked past them, then mounted his horse and rode away with three of his men behind him. Sarjya stood there for a long time, the dust raised by the horses' hooves swirling around him; then he sighed and turned back with his friends.

Chapter 17

To the children, waiting for details of the investigation into the sword tossed away by the Englishmen, it seemed like aeons had passed since they last had any new information. Prajakta had pleaded with Rama not to tell anyone about Sarjya's rash behaviour, especially Tukoji. As it is, he couldn't fathom why the Naikwadi gang had been called to Raigad, and would not hesitate to convince Aaisaheb they were more trouble than help.

As if in response to her not-so-polite thoughts, Shivaji's trusted aide suddenly loomed at their door, pressing his moustache down with his fingers and staring at each of them in turn. Distrust oozed from every pore as he regarded the children coldly, the afternoon sun reflecting off his earrings to make patterns on the walls.

"He's looking as if he wants to murder us! Are you sure he doesn't know what I did?" Sarjya whispered.

"Yes, Rama Tai promised! Now keep quiet," Prajakta answered.

"Ahem!" Tukoji began, "The sword we found was a poorly made replica of the Bhavani Talwar, complete with the scabbard and fake jewels stuck on it. It was similar in length and colour to our King's sword, but the resemblance could only have deceived a simpleton."

"Or someone who gave it only a cursory glance," Prajakta said. "Maybe they just wanted to delay the discovery of the theft?"

"Hmm, but if the plan was to steal the sword and replace it with this one, why did they suddenly throw the sword in direct view of the guards? What made them take the jewels instead? What we don't know is whether there are two sets of groups after the sword, or if the original plan was modified when Raje refused to meet the English," Tukoji said. "We have sent out men after the group who visited Raigad and made enquiries about the translator who accompanied them." He adjusted his cummerband and sniffed. "One of the Englishmen was seen talking to a man who rushed off inside the fort. No one can describe this person as he had wrapped a cloth around his face." Tukoji's clenched fists, by his side, conveyed what he wanted to do to this collaborator.

Sopan shifted restlessly, drawing a curious glance from Tukoji. "Er, Sir, can we get a look at the duplicate sword?" he asked.

"Why? In addition to being detectives, are you also an expert on swords?" Tukoji taunted.

Quick as a wink, Prajakta pushed Kaloo into Sarjya's lap so he got too busy trying to hold the squirming dog and couldn't react to Tukoji's words.

Sopan took care to keep his facial expression blank and spoke calmly, "No, sir, I'm just an ordinary boy, but my father is currently manufacturing swords with the new Spanish blade, and I have learnt a bit from him about metals and swords, so…"

Tukoji blinked to hide his surprise. "I …er… I… er… suppose there's no harm in showing this sword to you."

***

Shivaji Raje raised his palm, and the riders behind him halted. The King urged his white steed a few steps further into the clearing lined by dense bushes, his alert eyes taking in every detail of his surroundings. A crow cawed loudly from a nearby tree and, as if given a sign, Shivaji dismounted and walked into the forest.

Bhima, his trusted Mavala, stopped the men who wanted to follow him. "We need to wait here only," he said.

Shivaji quickly ducked past some low branches and walked right up to the bubbling brook; he looked around and mimicked the call of a mynah twice. Within moments, a similar sound emerged from the other side of the water, and a bent-over old man in crumpled saffron robes emerged. Leaning heavily on his stick, he tottered to the King and peered into his face. Then he straightened and beamed, revealing his youthful status.

"How goes it, Surya?" Shivaji asked.

"All quiet, my King. Aurangzeb has been simmering with rage since he heard about the plan for the Coronation. His ministers are wary of his foul temper and are avoiding unnecessary meetings. My man inside his court says there have been mutterings, ultimatums, and even threats of beheadings, but not even a whisper of any new attack in our area."

"So, you didn't hear of any plans for a mounted campaign," Shivaji twirled his moustache and said, "but are there any undercurrents of plots or schemes to create obstacles for the Coronation? Aurangzeb has always been a bit wary of Aai Bhavani's blessings on us. He derives malicious happiness by striking at our religion and beliefs. He could shift from targeting temples to going after our prized artefacts – after all, he hates everything sacred in Hindu culture."

"Both he and Adil Shah are intolerant." Surya spat onto the ground next to his feet. "No God but Allah, it seems! Raje, if there is any nefarious conspiracy to go after the Bhavani, it has to be from Bijapur. Theft and poison have always been the trademarks of the Begum of Adil Shah; she was as sly as her favourite Afzal Khan was all brute force!"

Shivaji nodded and thumped his man back on his back. "Thank you, stay safe. We'll meet in a fortnight; I'll tell you where and when through our usual messenger." He watched the daring fellow vanish into the trees beyond the brook, then looked skyward and prayed, "Aai Bhavani, protect our brave men!"

***

Sopan examined the duplicate scabbard, grimacing, "Such crude work, almost as if someone made it in a hurry."

"Perhaps they had to devise a plan quickly and got even lesser time to implement it?" Sarjya said.

"Or there were no craftsmen to do quality work since all of them are here working on Raje's Throne and umbrella," Prajakta ventured.

Tukoji nodded. "That's more likely." A gleam of respect showed in his eyes. "Our goldsmiths tell us this sword is only plated with a very thin layer of gold, not pure gold at all."

Sopan drew the sword out with a swish, and they all backed away warily. "This is so light, even I can wield it easily. Raje's sword is much heavier… and this is a narrow blade." His lower lip curled. "How on earth did they think anyone would get fooled? Our King's Bhavani has a broader cutting blade."

"I'm beginning to agree this was a makeshift thing, a way to muddy the waters or perhaps create confusion and distract us just enough for the thief to escape," Tukoji looked at Prajakta as he spoke.

Sopan ran his fingers over the hilt. "The stones are obviously coloured glass – anyone can tell that. And the carving – even our noblemen have swords with more intricate details than this shoddy workmanship!"

Tukoji permitted himself the tiniest of smiles before speaking, "Boy, can you tell where this blade was made from the metal used?"

"The English use a superior quality of Damascus steel as do the Spanish makers; this blade is greyer and rougher – I think it's locally made." Sopan nodded to himself. He peered closely at the hilt. "There are some tiny markings here," he said excitedly.

Tukoji bent to check before commenting, "This is not Urdu or Sanskrit. I will take it to the pundits and confirm; maybe we'll learn about the origins. Come!" He beckoned Sopan to accompany him, and both of them left with the sword.

"Tai?"

"What is it, Ganya?" Prajakta turned to look at Ganya, who was fidgeting with a thread on his kurta.

"I… was thinking… could I visit Raje's tailor and watch him at work? All those silks and gleaming gold threads for embroidery – his workshop must be a beautiful place!" His eyes shone as he asked, "Please, can I go? Maybe I can learn something and grow up to be like him," A shadow crossed his face. "No one would dare mock the King's tailor, surely."

Prajakta ruffled his hair; she missed the days when Ganya used to be supremely confident in even the most garish of clothes. Looking at his gaunt face and the dark circles that had appeared under his eyes, she sighed. "Sure, Ganya, let's ask Rama Tai."

"I'll go and find her!" He beamed and ran off.

Prajakta looked over at Sarjya, quietly whispering in Kaloo's ear, "You didn't go with Ganya? Why are you so quiet? Are you unwell?"

He shook his head and said, "Just trying to stay calm and quiet and not go jumping around with everyone. Besides, he needs to be a little less of a scaredy cat – he's been stuck to my side since we came here – not like the old Ganya who ran ahead of even me sometimes in his desperation for adventure! Let him go alone, he'll realize not everyone is out to mock him or hurt him."

Prajakta's eyebrows nearly touched her hairline at this display of restraint by Sarjya. "If you say so! Let's sit peacefully then, the two of us, and talk about something other than the theft; we've been obsessed by that ever since we got here."

"I've always wanted to be like Shivaji..." Sarjya said and sighed, his eyes on Kaloo happily chasing his tail.

"And now?" Prajakta had never seen her brother so pensive.

"Learning about his problems and worries, especially how he has so many enemies out to get him, has made me grateful for my normal life as well as more respectful of our King; he leads such a tough life with tremendous dignity and has sacrificed so much for us all!" Sarjya looked shamefaced. "I can never, even in many births, be like him; better to stop trying."

Prajakta looked at her downcast brother, his wavy hair falling over his eyes, his impish smile totally obliterated from his face. *What would Baba say?* she asked herself. *How would he cheer up Sarjya while encouraging him to keep being sensible?* She sucked in her cheeks then exhaled. "Sarjya, you are still very young, *re*! Our King is the greatest person you can emulate, but you are still a child...stop trying to act like a man. Baba always says, *Thembe thembe tale sache.* You have to take little steps before you can run. You can begin now by trying to stay positive in tough situations like Shivaji Raje and working on your skills."

Sarjya frowned. "I have no skills!"

Prajakta clicked her tongue and said, "Not everyone needs to apprentice with a craftsman. Helping Baba in the fields will make your body stronger in addition to providing for your family and village; grazing the cows will teach you about the terrain, preparing you for the guerrilla warfare our Mavalas are so adept at. Whatever you do, do it sincerely, and you will already be on your way to being like your hero! It wasn't the slicing of the finger to take the oath of Swarajya that you needed to copy; it was the idea of never letting outsiders rule over us – of fighting for our Motherland – that you needed to engrain. Focus on the idea, not the symbol!" Prajakta smiled and decided to end her speech; she knew her brother's patience was beginning to run out, like it did when Baba droned on about herbs and decoctions. She left him there, pondering about life, and playing fetch with Kaloo with a ball of rags.

Prajakta hummed to herself as she smoothed the bedsheets and folded the bedding. The rooms in Raigad were very comfortable, and the food was rich and lip-smackingly delicious, but she missed Aai's simple cooking and the sheer joy of listening to her parents talk about their day; their soft conversation acted as a lullaby to the children each night. Here, even amidst the sound of utensils being washed and the workers calling out to each other, it felt too quiet. She prayed to Lord Mahadev to help them solve the mystery of the missing jewels quickly. She did want to help the Queen Mother, but she also wanted to go back home to simpler problems. Prajakta paused; should they have investigated Tukoji also? In all the excitement that followed the discovery of the money and flowers in the guard's room, and then the fake sword, they hadn't had time to spy on Tukoji. She sighed, maybe it was for the best – he did appear to be thawing to their presence – she could have sworn he actually smiled at her once.

Rama Tai peeped in. "There you are! Sarjya was in his room, giving a very serious lecture to Kaloo about learning to sit quietly and to work on sincerity! Where are the other two?" she asked Prajakta.

"Sopan left with Tukoji to talk to someone who could read the inscriptions on the duplicate sword," Sarjya spoke up from behind her.

"*Arre*, how softly you crept up behind me! And where is Ganya?" Rama asked.

Prajakta sat up, a flicker of unease running down her spine. "Didn't he meet you? He wanted to visit the tailor."

"No, I was with Aaisaheb all this while," Rama said. "He must have asked someone else for directions to Ganpat's workshop. Has he been gone long?"

Prajakta rubbed the gooseflesh on her arms. *Something was wrong!* "Yes, it's been quite some time."

Chapter 18

Tukoji and Sopan returned from their visit to the translator and pundits, bursting with news, but the panic and fear they saw on Prajakta and Rama's faces made them forget what they were going to say. The worried group raced down the steps into the courtyard and then to Ganpat, the tailor's workshop. They found the man knee deep in bales of silk.

He looked up at the clatter the large group made on the cobblestones and frowned, his proboscis-like nose making him look both foreboding and funny.

"Ganpat!" Rama gasped, "Have you seen Ganya?"

The slender man rose from the floor with a groan. "Who? Who are you talking about?"he asked.

"A boy… like me!" Sarjya pushed his way to the front and said. "He's… he's almost as tall as me, but slightly fairer and… and he has a crooked lower tooth. He was coming to find you!"

"Me?" The tailor rubbed his fingers and wiped them on his leggings. "But why? Did he want something stitched? I really have no time – so many clothes to get ready for the ceremonies ahead and-"

"No, no," Prajakta butted in, "he was interested in all the expensive brocade and silks you have, and in learning about how you make clothes for our King. He was coming here to meet you."

Ganpat shook his head and said, "No boy came here. I have been here since morning. He must have gone somewhere else or gotten lost; children that age get distracted easily."

"Yes, that's more likely," Tukoji agreed. "Let's spread out and look for him." He strode to the nearest rampart and shouted for two guards to come over; he sent one with Sarjya and told the other to go in the opposite direction with Sopan. Tukoji, himself, moved towards the new hall while Prajakta and Rama headed to the upper rooms in the fort.

Prajakta gave one last look around the tailor's workshop in the fervent hope that Ganya would jump out from behind a bale of cloth and yell, '*Surprise!*' but all she saw was Ganpat's bent head and unusually long nose as he cut the white silk cloth, perhaps for the King's robes. The thick hair on his head was plastered to his scalp with sweat. Shifting those bundles must be hard work, Prajakta thought to herself. The man had a small bandage on two of his fingers. I wonder how he injured himself, she frowned. After all, he must be spending all his time with soft cloth and threads, not doing any labour. Aah, yes… Rama Tai had mentioned he does sword practice too! She felt a pang of sympathy for the poor man and his tragic story.

Three hours later, Prajakta and Rama were on the verge of tears, and Sopan was sitting with his head in his hands. Sarjya paced up and down the room, muttering, with Kaloo at his heels, "Where could Ganya have gone? Why did he go alone? Why did I have to choose that moment only to bolster his self-confidence? It's all my fault, I abandoned my friend!" His shoulders drooped. Then, he looked up and said, "Tai, did you check Raje's chambers and the inner room – the one with his clothes and turbans and jewels? Ganya was fascinated by that place; he would have lived there forever if he could! Perhaps he-"

"Yes, Sarjya, we looked there too." Prajakta bit her lower lip to keep from crying; she was the oldest – she needed to stay calm and positive – but what would she tell Ganya's parents? The Naikwadi children had been chuffed to come to Raigad. Their King needed them; they had thought themselves so intelligent, and look where that had got them. They were nowhere close to solving the mystery, and now their friend was missing! Prajakta's stomach lurched; this felt just like when that scar-faced villain had kidnapped Sarjya. Where could Ganya have disappeared to? Had he fallen somewhere in an isolated part of the fort, unable to cry out for help? Had he been taken like Sarjya? But why? They still hadn't the faintest idea where the jewels were. Prajakta's mind raced in all directions till she developed a splitting headache.

Sarjya and Sopan continued to search late into the evening with lanterns. 'Ganya, Ganya,' they kept shouting, with Kaloo adding barks and sniffing detours as his contribution. The rose-tinged sun sank into the horizon, and lamps began to be lit all over the fort and in the valley deep below, but the Naikwadi children couldn't find any sign of their friend. One by one, every able-bodied man and woman picked up a torch and joined the search party, but it was as if the earth had swallowed up the boy.

"Saheb?"

"What is it?" Tukoji whirled, the torch in his hand sputtering in the air.

"Someone near the marketplace told me they saw a small boy moving alone towards Takmak Tok." the man said.

Tukoji hissed. Takmak Tok! Why would Ganya go there? He had explained to the children on the very first day that they must steer clear of the place, and that it was a steep drop from there, hundreds of feet of sheer rock. Every man, woman and child in Raigad already knew how dangerous it was, even in broad daylight… he looked around at the darkening sky and shuddered. To go there in the darkness, alone, without a torch, and no knowledge of the topography, was suicidal! Tukoji gulped, then came to a decision. "Call all the guards on duty here. We need to form a search party."

An hour later, 10 men held their torches as high as they could, but even then, they could see only a few feet into the dense undergrowth below. They had shouted themselves hoarse on the path to the sheer drop. There was no sign anyone had been here recently.

"Sardar, we can't see anything!"

"I know that!" Tukoji snapped, at his wits' end. What would he tell Aaisaheb? How would he face the other children? Why on Earth had that blasted boy come here? Did he find a clue that led him here? Tukoji gasped as if someone had thrown icy water on him. Could Ganya have come upon the thief, and did that person drag him here? Tukoji stared into the shadows below, his ears straining for a sound, a cry, anything. But only the hoot of an owl pierced the ominous silence. His shoulders sagged. "Let's go back. It's too dark to search. We'll come back tomorrow at first light with more men and ropes." They trudged back to the marketplace, where a frantic Moropant was waiting for them. Tukoji met the Minister's eyes, shook his head, and the two made their way to inform their King.

"*Muli*!"

Prajakta felt a hand on her shoulder. "Aaisaheb!" She jumped up and bowed before the Queen Mother. She had just been asking Rama the latest news.

The graceful Queen first looked at Rama sternly, as if asking her if Prajakta knew about the futile search at Takmak Tok. The maid pressed her lips together and shook her head. Aaisaheb sat down and told the girl to do the same. She said, "Rama told me that Ganya is missing… I wanted to come here specifically to talk to you, just like your own mother would. I know you are all very disturbed, but this is not a time for fear or panic. I believe in you – you must make the best use of your instincts and keen mind to search for clues. It's too much of a coincidence that your friend disappears just a few days after the theft! My experience tells me that the two are definitely linked. Take a deep breath, clear your mind of all thoughts, and then begin again with a calm, logical approach. I'm definite you can solve this puzzle."

Prajakta looked at her Queen's tranquil face and kind eyes, and felt immeasurably better. All would be well; they would find a way out.

Getting to her feet, Aaisaheb patted Prajakta's back and said, "I have to go and supervise the order of marigolds for the ceremony – only 10 days to go now! But Rama will be at hand to help in any way she can. I don't think anyone can sleep peacefully tonight till our Ganya is found." The Queen Mother departed with a rustle of silks, leaving behind a faint smell of sandalwood.

"*Attar*!" Prajakta slapped her forehead. "We forgot to follow up on that!" She turned to Rama and asked, "Are there any shops in the fort that sell attar?"

"No, no one uses it much amongst our people," Rama answered.

"Then where would one get it from?"

The sombre woman closed her eyes and thought. "A travelling salesman visits now and then, but we all buy incense for prayers from him – no one can afford perfumes. Besides, all of us associate attar with the Mughals and prefer not to use it."

"Where does Aaisaheb get her sandalwood from?" Prajakta persisted.

"There is a very old tree by the side of the Gangasagar lake near the Rani Mahal," Rama said, pointing to the right. "Aaisaheb's attendant has the responsibility of making a fresh paste every day at dawn for her prayers and daily use."

"So, no one else has access to it? Hmmm, have you ever smelled the stronger, sweeter version of it from any of the women – the attendants, the Queen's maidens, even the milkmaids, vegetable sellers or dancers?" Prajakta refused to be defeated.

"Hmmm, not really." Rama tilted her head to one side, then her eyes widened. "I smelled it once, on Chandra!"

"Chandra – that name again! She is Soyarabai's maid, right?"

Rama nodded. "It was only once, and I was surprised since she is a Hindu, but she brushed it off with a laugh and a blush, saying she brought it from a passing merchant. She kept saying she hated it and had used only one drop before the bottle broke. Good riddance, she had said. I remember she went red and giggled that it still smelled even after a dip in the pond."

"Could she ever have been in the weapons room?' Prajakta asked.

"She definitely could have been there with Soyarabaisaheb before the theft, but that wouldn't have been suspicious – she goes everywhere her mistress goes," Rama rolled her eyes and continued, "and fancies herself just as royal too! Yesterday, she even wore a pair of silver anklets. All the other maids were out of their minds with jealousy, but she told them Rani Soyara gave them to her as a reward for her services, and they all shut up; after all, the poor thing has no one of her own. We all thought her mistress must have pitied her and got the anklets for Chandra when she bought stuff for herself for the Grand Coronation."

Prajakta stood up and dusted her skirts, mindful of the darkening shadows. "I need to call Sarjya and Kaloo; they've been searching for hours without a break. Sarjya! Where are you?" She shook her head, muttering, "That boy goes into all corners of the fort and eavesdrops on people! Even in Naikwadi-"

"What is it, Prajakta?" Rama shook the girl, who was now standing as if turned to stone.

"The anklet! The woman… poison!" Prajakta's voice grew shriller with every word. "Sarjya overheard her say something about poison. She's Rani Soyara's maid; could she have poisoned Sambhaji Raje? Could that be the reason he fell ill?"

Rama gasped. "And so Ranisaheb could not attend to Raje, and he was alone in his chambers that day! But," she stopped, excitement fading from her eyes, and asked, "but so what? What was the reason Raje needed to be alone?"

Prajakta pursed her lips and tried to think, but came up blank. "Maybe we should tell Aaisaheb all this and talk to Chandra. That will surely lead us to the next step."

The two raced down the passageway, nearly bumping into Sopan.

"Did you find Ganya?" Prajakta asked, "And where are Sarjya and Kaloo?"

"Sarjya was hungry so we ate first – he's still finishing but..." Sopan's face fell. "We didn't find Ganya."

"Ganya must be so hungry! He never could tolerate hunger… except in the last few months… he seemed to be eating much less than usual. His clothes had begun to hang off his body." A tear ran down Prajakta's cheeks, and she whispered, "Only Mahadev knows what condition he must be in!"

"We will find him!"

Prajakta's jaw dropped at the imperious voice. Rama bowed, and the children followed suit. Shivaji Raje was here, in their room!

The King met each of their eyes in turn; his dark, serious gaze remained their sole focal point amid the flickering of the torches in the room. He said, "We have closed all entry and exit points. No one can enter or leave Raigad for any reason. We have spoken to the guards at the Maha Darwaza – they report they are sure no one has left the fort. Ganya has to be inside Raigad. We will find him!" Shivaji's eyes blazed with fury and his rage echoed in the small space, "Whoever has done this will be severely punished."

"Er, Sir?" Rama hesitated. "Can you come with us to the Queen Mother's chambers? We need to tell you something!"

Chapter 19

The Maratha King paced up and down, up and down; his turban had been deposited on a chair along with his pearls and earrings. It was as if he wanted to be free of at least some of the burdens he carried. At the other end of the room was the bed where Rama knelt, pressing Aaisaheb's feet. Prajakta, Sopan, Sarjya and Kaloo sat in between the two towering personalities, mutely looking from one to the other, waiting.

"Here she is, Sir!" The guard pushed Chandra into the room.

"You! You gave my son poison!" Shivaji's rage was palpable as he moved in on the woman cowering on the floor.

Prajakta caught a quick glimpse of the Queen's maid – her sharp-features and dusky looks set her apart from the other servants; there was something magnetic about her. She had a smug, arrogant expression, almost as if she were proud of what she had done.

"Stop Shivba!" Aaisaheb pulled him away and said, "Let me speak to her." She signalled to Rama, who quickly led the children out of the room.

"But Rama Tai!" Sarjya had to be dragged out, protesting, "I want to hear what she says."

"So do we all, boy, but this is a matter for the elders," she said as she hustled them all down the winding steps and back to their rooms.

"Rama!" one of the guards on the way called out.

She turned around and moved closer for a closer look at the man's face. "It's you, Shankar! How are you? How old is your baby now?"

The huge man beamed and said, "She is three months old and a constant delight. I hoped I'd meet you. With all the comings and goings on, I completely forgot to ask if Ganpat, the tailor, found his golden thimble?"

Rama frowned. "Golden thimble? What do you mean?" she asked.

The guard glanced at the children and Kaloo curiously before replying, "Three or four days ago, Ganpat came to me, wringing his hands; he had lost his golden thimble and was desperate to find it. He told me he was certain he had left it inside Raje's room when he measured him for the ceremonial robes the previous day."

"Then what happened?'

"Naturally, I refused to let him go inside alone, but he was in tears, saying that was all he had left of his great teacher in Indore. All of us laugh at his appearance behind his back, though I know we shouldn't; after all, his son… anyway, I felt bad for him, and I let him inside for just a few moments."

"Did he enter the weapons room?" Prajakta asked.

Shankar bristled. "How could I let him do that? Ganpat stayed in sight, even in Raje's bedroom. He said he needed to look under the bed in case the thimble had rolled there. I remained standing beyond him, inside the bedroom, to make sure no one went to the inner rooms. He moved around some chairs in the outer meeting hall and looked around on the floor, even the walls!" He laughed. "Then he said he didn't find it, and left."

"This was the day after the theft?"

"No, it was two days after that on Thursday, when Raje's men had combed each room to make sure the jewels were definitely not in his chambers."

"Were your eyes on him all the time?"

Rama looked at Prajakta with a frown. *Why was she asking all these questions about the tailor? So what if he had entered the royal chambers – it wasn't before the theft was discovered, so it was alright.*

Shankar's complexion reddened as he pressed his lips together. "When he was searching, someone shouted from below, and I ran to the window of the bedroom to look out, but there was no one there." His eyes implored Rama before he spoke, "But Ganpat didn't go inside the weapon's room at all. I swear on my life he was only in the bedroom!"

Sarjya began to see the connection. "Ganya was going to meet the tailor when he vanished; he is involved in all this! He… he…," he said, his face turning red, "he's done something to Ganya!" He turned and sprinted for the man's workshop.

"Wait for us!" Prajakta chased after him with Sopan and Kaloo.

Rama looked around frantically; only one other guard was in the hallway, mouth hanging open at the antics of the children. "Come with us," she tugged at his arm and urged, "bring all the men you can on the way!"

When they had last been in Ganpat's workshop, it had been neatly ordered, with small boxes of lace, zari, needles and thread. There had even been paintings on the wall. Prajakta remembered the drawings of extravagantly dressed nobles and members of the royal households of the Shinde, Gaikwad, and Bhosale families – but now the place lay in shambles. "Someone was in a great hurry to pack up here," Tukoji noted, "the expensive stuff like gold zari and the special silk we ordered for the canopy has been taken. And his sewing tools are gone too!"

Prajakta gazed around and said, "Someone surely must have noticed. Why didn't they stop him?"

"Why would they have any reason to, child? Anyone has a right to pack up the contents of his own shop after all. He may just have been in a hurry to get home."

"I just know that man had something to do with the theft!" Sarjya insisted. "Why would he vanish at exactly this time?" Kaloo nosed around the scattered material and whined. "What it is... what is it, boy?" Sarjya asked. There was a small pot in a corner of the workshop with some thick grey material. Sarjya dragged it outside into the light, dipped a finger into it and sniffed. "Sopan, smell this! Isn't this similar to the lime and sand mixture your father used to make when he repaired his workshop after the Mughals destroyed it?"

Tukoji went back into the room to look at the walls again. "No obvious repairs seem to have been done here recently," he scratched his head, then gasped, "the material in Raje's outer chamber was just like this! What on earth was Ganpat planning to do with it?"

"Sardar, Sardar!" A gaping Mavala stood at the door. "Aaisaheb and Raje have called you all to his chambers."

"What is it?" Tukoji asked.

"I don't know, Sir. I was just ordered to give you this message."

The children were hot on Tukoji's heels; they all tumbled into the room together, where Shivaji and Aaisaheb stood, surrounded by their guards. On the arrival of the children, the men parted to reveal a sobbing boy on the carpet.

"Ganya!" Sarjya dropped to his knees to hug his friend. "You are back!"

A beaming Prajakta moved forward, her smile faltering at the boy's bedraggled appearance; he had a cut on his lower lip and a black eye. "What happened? Did you fall? How did you get hurt?" she asked.

Ganya looked at her and cried harder. The Queen Mother urged him to sit by her side on the bed. She wiped his tears and hugged him. "It's all okay, my child, no one can hurt you now."

"Who did this to you?" Sarjya's expression was murderous.

"That... that tailor!" Ganya's feeble voice emerged through his tears.

"I knew it!" Sarjya clenched his fist. "That monster! He hit my friend and kidnapped him" He turned to Shivaji and asked, "Did you catch him and put him in chains?"

A muscle flickered at the corner of the King's jaw. "He has vanished. My men found the boy in an isolated part of the dungeons that hasn't been used for years."

The dungeons! They gasped and turned to look at Ganya again. Becoming aware of his moment in the spotlight, he sat straighter and wiped his cheeks before looking around at the King's chambers in awe.

Over the next few minutes, they learned that Ganya had been too impatient to look for Rama; he had seen a worker carrying onions and asked him for directions to the tailor's shop. When he found the workshop empty, Ganya decided to wait there. "The place was full of exquisite zari and beads, and I couldn't resist touching them!" he told them. "There was even one shiny red bale of cloth just like the shirt I've always wanted. I bent to look at it and heard voices coming from somewhere. No one was visible; then I crouched and realized there was a secret room below me! I could hear a faint conversation – I nearly had to lie flat to hear them speak. Two men were talking about the stolen jewels from the Bhavani Sword and how to smuggle them out of the fort. I realized I was in danger and tried to leave, but before I could, a hidden door in the floor slid open, and two men emerged, one with an unusually long nose." Ganya bit his lip, then winced at the pain.

"I froze for just a moment, and then, when I tried to run, the other man – a taller and heftier fellow with a thick beard – caught hold of my arm and twisted it behind my back." Ganya sobbed at the remembered pain, then the tiniest of smiles broke through before he said, "but I've lost so much weight *na,* so my clothes have become loose! I managed to wriggle out of the sleeve of my kurta, and I had nearly broken free when the long-nosed fellow grabbed me and punched me in the face… I passed out!" Ganya looked at the loving faces around him and found the strength to continue, "When I came to, they were discussing how to get rid of me."

There was a sudden silence as Ganya stopped telling his story. *How could they hit a child like that?* Aaisaheb had a grim look on her face while Shivaji's right hand tightened on his sword.

"And then?" Sarjya asked.

"Then they stuffed rags in my mouth and bundled me into a sack. I couldn't see anything… I must have fainted again or something, because when I opened my eyes, I was in a dark place with no windows and," the boy shuddered and said, "mice were scampering around. I shouted and cried and howled. Still, no one could hear me. I was ravenous and cold and smelly because I peed myself." Ganya's face turned sheepish as he continued, "I was terrified of never being found and dying of hunger." He turned to Shivaji Raje and asked, "Did my mimicry work?"

The King grasped the string of pearls around his neck and said, "One of my men noted the dust around the entrance to an abandoned part of the underground dungeons had been disturbed; he went down the broken steps and heard a faint sound." Shivaji's smile broadened as he continued, "he told us it sounded as if there was a mad elephant down there! The terrified man ran to tell his mates. His leader sent out more men with plenty of torches, and they found you in one of the old prisons."

Ganya nodded, pleased with himself. "The rags in my mouth made it difficult to shout, but I could make some sounds, and I thought an elephant sound from the dungeons would most definitely be investigated!" He sniffed the air and sat up straighter. A heavenly fragrance of varan bhaat entered the room before the maid who was carrying it. "Food!" Ganya beamed, reaching for the plate before giving Aaisaheb and Shivaji an endearing grin. "May I?"

"Of course, my boy!" They both said together and laughed. *First things first!*

Chapter 20

That night, none of the children could sleep peacefully. Prajakta insisted that they all be in the same room so she could keep an eye on Ganya. The poor boy moaned in pain till dawn, unable to sleep comfortably in any position; and, when he did doze off, he'd have nightmares and wake up screaming. Prajakta had swiftly made up a paste of marigold leaves and *haldi,* and applied it to Ganya's black eye and split lip. The traumatized boy had kept muttering about wanting to change his name. As if sensing his fear, Kaloo had deposited himself at Ganya's side, raising his head every few minutes to look at the boy with thoughtful eyes, as if to ensure all was well.

After a night-long vigil, Prajakta had a quick bath at dawn and tiptoed to her restless friend. "No signs of fever, thank the Goddess!" she whispered to herself as she walked back from the kitchen with hot milk for the boys. Rama arrived shortly afterwards with fruits for them, and Prajakta marvelled at how well turned out she was at all hours of the day. Since the first time they had met, Prajakta had found herself trying to emulate the graceful, soft-spoken woman. She stole a look at the vermillion *kunkoo* on Rama's forehead, and noted her toe rings and the black beads around her neck. *So, she's married now!* She hadn't been when they had met with her father at Rajgad. Prajakta tilted her head and watched Rama bending to comfort Ganya; she didn't appear too unhappy with her lot – in fact, she glowed with a quiet pride. Hmm, Prajakta thought, maybe she didn't marry a total stranger who stifled her personality.

"Prajakta," Rama said, "last night Raje sent his men in all directions; they found evidence that Ganpat and his friend are travelling south, possibly in the direction of Bijapur. Also, Chandra broke down and confessed that Ganpat had a friend, Ahmed, who had been living with him. The man would stay hidden most of the day and roam around the fort freely in the darkness. She bumped into him when Queen Soyarabai had sent her out to collect some flowers which only bloomed at night. She fell for the tall, muscular man who promised to marry her. Besotted by him and his gifts of gold and perfumes, Chandra agreed to slip something into some of Shambhu Raje's food; she swears he told her it wasn't dangerous, and would only make the Prince ill for a couple of days."

"But why did he want Sambhaji out of the way?" Prajakta wondered.

"Not Shambhu Raje; his plan was for Rani Soyara to stay with the Prince out of concern, ensuring Raje would be alone when Ganpat came to measure him for his special Coronation robes."

"Rama Tai, then what was he planning to do?" Sarjya rubbed the sleep from his eyes.

"I don't know, *bala*. Chandra knew only her part of the task; Tukoji and Moropant are putting together the other pieces of the puzzle, especially now that we know the Adil Shahi is behind this," Rama answered.

Prajakta set out a bowl of milk for Kaloo, who had joined his master. "Go," she nudged her brother, who seemed ready to bend down and lap at the milk himself. "At least freshen up first!"

"Rama Tai, today, can we go look at the main hall being decorated for the Coronation?" Sarjya asked before getting up and folding his bedding.

"Sure!" She brightened. "That will be perfect for today; something to take our minds off all these plots and plans." She turned to Ganya and said, "and Aaisaheb has kept new clothes to be given to all of you."

"Ganpat didn't stitch them, na? I won't wear them even if," Ganya gulped and whispered, "if they are of silk and zari, and in all the colours in the world!"

The children turned to Rama and chorused, "We also don't…"

"No, no, children! Ganpat made clothes only for the Royal Family; we have other tailors in Raigad, too! You'll just love the garments, and this tailor too."

"I hope he has a small nose and is very short and plump!" Ganya's statement had them all laughing loudly.

Nearby, in Shivaji Raje's chambers, the meeting of the Council of Ministers was growing heated. The King couldn't understand how Ganpat had managed to put together such an elaborate plan, and set it in motion without anyone becoming suspicious. The fact that an outsider like Ahmed lived for days inside the fort and was never discovered made him livid; it was as if the Adil Shahi had been able to strike at the very heart of the Maratha Empire, and now, with thousands of people and hundreds of guests expected within a week, was Raigad going to be safe enough from his ever-increasing enemies?

"My King," Moropant Pingale said with a morose expression on his face, "Our spies have reached Indore and are inquiring into Ganpat's antecedents, especially his mentor, who was known to the Shinde family." His lips drooped at his next words. "It appears Ganpat was indeed a highly skilled and well-trained craftsman, but now we are learning he was greedy and under suspicion of having pocketed a few pearls from the Maharani's collection. The references he gave made no mention of it, as they had never been able to prove he did it."

The Queen Mother watched her exhausted son's face grow darker at their lapses in security, and shaking her head, she said, "Shivba, as your stature grows, your inner circle needs to be secure and trustworthy. We need to ensure our capital, Raigad, has only the most loyal and proven people within the perimeter of the fort. We need to learn a lesson from this incident and doubly verify every piece of information." She looked around at the men by her son's side and warned, "Each of us needs to be extra careful in the coming few days. Our enemies are looking to destabilize our security and threaten this era of peaceful Swarajya." She turned to Tukoji. "What have you found out about the so-called Bhavani imitation?"

"Aai...," Tukoji's high-pitched voice never failed to make Moropant choke a smile. "Aaisaheb," he continued after a dirty look at the Chief Minister, "it appears the Englishmen were somehow hoping to substitute it for the real thing. How they thought they would even get near the Bhavani is a mystery."

Raje stopped pacing the room. "You say the maker engraved his name on the blade, and our experts say it's the English script?"

"Yes, my Lord."

"Hmm," Shivaji stroked his beard as he talked, "isn't it strange that there were two simultaneous plots involving the Bhavani Sword? I don't believe in coincidences!" He turned to Moropant. "What proof do we have that the men who wanted to meet me were English?"

The Minister was flummoxed. "Er, they said they were!"

Shivaji raised an eyebrow, and Moropant realized what his King meant. 'Always verify' was going to become the new motto after these mishaps. The King said, "So, if the wily Bijapuri players had paid goras to act like Englishmen, and got the sword maker to engrave a few letters in English on the blade, what was their motive? Was the fake sword just a distraction while Ganpat and his partner got away with the jewels? Or had the two men initially planned to substitute the imitation sword for the real one, and then had to make do with the stones only when that plan could not be implemented?"

With no answers coming readily, Shivaji adjourned the meeting for the day. Once the men had left, he walked to the weapons room and unsheathed the Bhavani. He sighed as he ran his fingers over the hilt. *With just a week to go for the Coronation, should he replace the jewels? It would be a mammoth task to get good-quality gemstones of that size at such short notice, but it could still be done.* He decided to summon the royal goldsmith the next day to discuss the situation. Shivaji Bhosale believed in being prepared for all eventualities.

Elsewhere in the palace, the children were having an infinitely better day. Resplendent in their new clothes, they set out on a tour of the nearly ready Grand Hall. The Coronation was to take place here, and hundreds of workers were frantically adding finishing touches to the large pillars that supported the huge Darbar. Rama unrolled some of the beautiful carpets that lay ready for display for the next week to show them the intricate patterns and gorgeous colours. Many of the chandeliers were already up, the sunrays reflecting off them into a rainbow of hues. Sarjya rubbed his neck and grimaced; all that craning to look up at the beautiful pearl strings and awning of luxurious gold cloth had pleasantly tired the children. Looking around, he noticed the notorious mouse-catcher Jilbya making his tortuous way to where Kaloo was happily chewing on a piece of wood. The glint in the cat's eyes prompted Sarjya to move closer. Two workers carrying an ornate sculpture of Goddess Lakshmi were heading in the same direction from opposite sides of the hall. Sarjya shouted, "Look out!" just as Jilbya slapped Kaloo with his paw and set off a noisy squabble between dog and cat. The sculpture wobbled two or three times, but tragedy was averted.

"Must be the first time I prevented a disaster rather than caused it!" Sarjya ran his fingers through his hair and chuckled as the children and Rama ran up to pat him on the back.

"Things are turning around for you!" Prajakta beamed. "Hopefully, this is a good omen for our presence here, too."

One of the craftsmen beckoned them over to proudly show them the gold throne. It was the most beautiful thing the children had ever seen. "It's made from 32 maunds of gold," the man stated.

They all crowded around the magnificent centrepiece; even Ganya forgot his painful ordeal and ran his fingers lovingly over the velvet cushion seat. *Maybe they'd let him sit on it just once!* He looked around, then decided against asking. His love for beautiful things had nearly gotten him killed; he shuddered, better to watch from afar from now on.

"There will be a tiger skin over the seat at the actual ceremony," the artisan told them.

"Wow!" Sarjya tried to visualize the grand spectacle that would take place – thousands of people watching as their King took his place on the majestic throne, holding his sword aloft.... he frowned. *Would the jewels ever be returned? Could the Bhavani regain her brilliance? Lord Mahadev, please help us catch those villains before they reach Bijapur!*

Sopan had been quiet so far, but the sight of the eight gold pillars around the throne, which would support the canopy of gold embroidery, had him spellbound. "Such grandeur, such magnificent work. *Wah*!" he couldn't resist saying.

Rama told the craftsman, "His father is working on Spanish blades for swords, and Sopan here knows quite a bit about metals and moulding them."

"Is it?" The man was impressed and led the boy closer to point out the two large goldfish heads, the horse tails, and the pair of gold scales carved on either side of the throne.

Sopan's fingers traced the intricate carving. The sight of his large, stubby fingers on the delicate craftsmanship made him smile ruefully – this detailed work was too fine for him. But he would try to learn more about fashioning the best weapons in the land that would fit perfectly in the hands of their brave warriors. He was already learning to use the massive broadswords; surely that would give him insight into how to design better, lighter weapons. The Marathas weren't as tall as the Spanish, who had originally designed these brilliant weapons, so customizing the swords for their body type would aid them greatly in battle. Yes, he nodded to himself; he had found his calling. He would make his ancestors proud by carrying on the family legacy, but do it in his own unique way!

Chapter 21

Ganya remained morose the next day, shadowing Sarjya everywhere till even he got impatient. "*Arre,* I'll trip and fall. Walk a little further away from me, *na*!" he snapped. Ganya's face fell, making Sarjya feel ashamed. "What I meant to say is..."

"It's okay, Sarjya, I'll be more careful."

They couldn't possibly ask Ganya to remain alone in the room; he was terrified of the slightest noise, and so they took him everywhere they went. People from all over the fort kept dropping in to check on him and exclaim over his injuries, but the only time Ganya's mood lightened the slightest was when he was with his Naikwadi friends. Little by little, his appetite returned. In fact, surprisingly, now all he wanted to do was eat. Every few hours, he'd pile his plate with food and gulp down everything, all while staring into space.

"It's scary to watch him, it's as if he's making up for all those months of not eating!" Sarjya said. The brother and sister had taken some time out to talk amongst themselves, while Sopan and Kaloo stayed within Ganya's line of sight for reassurance. "Tai, do you think they'll send us back to Naikwadi now?" He threw a pebble down from the lookout point and watched it roll down the ravine.

"I think so; now the thief has been identified, and all they have to do is catch him," she said. "What more can we do here now?"

Sarjya ran his fingers over the rocky ledge, tracing the smooth joints and marvelling at the masons' expertise. "I wonder how Ganpat managed to wrench out the jewels, though. Raje says he measured him for clothes, fitted him for the ones he had already made, and then left. When did he get time to take the emerald, ruby and diamonds?" Prajakta stared at her brother, tracing designs on the stones, a frown marring her thoughtful expression. "What is it, Tai? Do I have something on my face?" he asked.

"The joints between the stones!" She tugged her plaits.

"These ones?" Sarjya looked down.

"No, the ones in Raje's chambers – they were scraped away to make space," she tapered off, "for something small!" Prajakta looked up with a new light in her eyes.

"Like the jewels!" Sarjya jumped up, causing the other two children and the dog to run over to investigate his excitement. "The crevice was the hiding place! But it was empty when we saw it."

"Yes," Prajakta said, "that was four days after the theft. Ganpat must have waited for the furore to die down and then removed them."

Sarjya clutched her arm, thrilled by the deduction. "That day when he came back for his thimble… supposedly!"

"And was lurking around near Raje's bed!" Ganya nodded excitedly.

"But Tai, why didn't he carry away the jewels at the same time as he removed them from the sword?" Ganya asked.

"Time!" Sopan nodded slowly. "Time fell short, or maybe someone came in suddenly or grew suspicious, and Ganpat thought he would be frisked on his way out, so he couldn't keep the jewels on him."

***

"My Lord!" Tukoji's right-hand man, Maloji, had an excited look on his face. "We managed to track down one of the *goras*."

Shivaji's eyes narrowed, "The ones who came to the fort that day?"

"Yes, Sir, he was in the English army, but was thrown out for theft and cheating."

Raje blew out air from his cheeks and followed his man to the holding cells.

"*Bol*!" One of the guards pushed the man to the ground just as Shivaji Raje walked in. The King frowned at his people and ordered them to open the man's shackles. Motioning to the interpreter to come forward, he asked him to tell the man he wasn't in any danger; all they wanted was information. The prisoner's white skin grew red and blotchy at the translated words, then a quick look of gratification crossed his face, and he began to speak – slowly at first, and then faster and louder.

"Sir, he says he was approached by a bearded man last week who offered him payment to join a group of people posing as an official English delegation. The man told him they would be given a time when you were definitely absent from the fort; they were to return after being refused entry at the gate, and given instructions to drop a package nearby in the full visibility of the watching guards."

The Englishman glanced up at the Maratha King and then lowered his gaze. He muttered a few words that had the translator straining to listen.

"Sir, he says he was handed the sack containing a long object and a golden cloth to cover it. They were to hold it aloft to the guards at the Maha Darwaja, then uncover and toss the sack as far into the valley as they could."

"I thought there was something fishy about that!" Shivaji's earrings jangled vigorously as his suspicions were confirmed. "So that's what it was – just a distraction and a ploy to get us to suspect the English." The

Maratha King looked at the downcast foreigner. "Let us try to catch Ganpat and his friend first; then, after this man identifies them, we can let him go."

***

Rama watched the children eat their lunch silently. "What is it? You all are so quiet today!" The kids looked at each other, then Sariya spoke, "Rama Tai, will we be going home now?"

She gave them a gentle smile and said softly, "Aaisaheb wants you to wait for a day; maybe the thieves will be intercepted before they reach Bijapur."

A clamour broke out outside, and the children stood up, eager to find out what was happening. Sopan emerged from the crowd with all the details. "The news of the jewel theft has spread all over the country; each person has their own version of things." They stared at the agitated residents of the fort.

A dark-complexioned, stocky man with a sparse moustache spoke loudly, "How can Shivaji be King without the Bhavani Sword? If the Devi gave it to him as a boon, she has now taken it away. He is not fit to be King!"

The Maratha warriors listening to this bristled; how dare someone talk like this? They advanced on the man who jumped onto a larger rock and shouted even louder, "Goddess Bhavani is angry at us all! She doesn't want Shivaji crowned as Emperor; if this ceremony still goes ahead, bad luck will befall the Maratha Kingdom. Mark my words, we will all be doomed!"

People gasped. The whispers began. *What was the man saying? Was he right? Was their King out of favour with the Gods?* The murmurs grew louder, and the stocky man moved quickly and disappeared in the crowd before anyone could stop him. Some of Shivaji's guards gave chase to the man, and the rest got busy trying to dispel people's concerns.

"Is it true?" an old woman asked. "Is the Bhavani missing?"

"No, Ajji, nothing like that," answered the guard.

Then another man pushed his way forward and asked, "What was that man saying about bad luck? Have we been cursed? Where is the Bhavani?"

Rama tried to remonstrate with a few wailing women, but the crowd was in no mood to listen, and she quickly backed off and pulled the children away with her.

Elsewhere in the state, the story was repeated in a similar fashion.

"It's all a very cleverly orchestrated plan!" Shivaji told Aaisaheb. "The Bijapuris have sent their spies to spread misinformation and convince the people we're in trouble; they want to dampen their enthusiasm for the Coronation and sow doubts about our army's ability to continue to win. This is just the next phase of their scheme, you've got to admire their sheer effrontery!"

The Queen Mother was disgusted. "That's how they ruled for so long."

"Don't worry, Mother, our men are going from village to village and dispelling the rumours, we're even calling the headmen of each village with his family for the ceremony next week to confirm for themselves that all is as it was. These people will then go back and reassure everyone that all is well."

"Will the new stones be set by then, Shivba?" Jeejabai asked.

The King gave the elderly monarch a smile. "The gems should be here by then, but I am still hopeful of getting our original ones back."

The Queen Mother glanced at him and asked, "Are you getting superstitious too, son?"

He let out a slow chuckle. "No, no, mother! I believe in our cause, and that is enough to fuel me in my crusade; but all the same, I'd like to foil the dastardly plan of these Adil Shahi plotters, and recover the original ruby and emerald."

"Isn't it interesting how they made sure the total number of missing jewels was 13?" Jeejabai remarked with a smile.

"Maybe an unlucky number for them, not me!" the King's earrings danced as he said.

"But an interesting psychological game they are playing."

He nodded. "Maybe we need to take a few tips from them. Now, the only mystery left to solve is when did Ganpat wrench off the stones? I feel restless when I think about that day – what did I miss – how did he get out the gems from under my very eyes? To think we never suspected Ganpat! Did he give us no clue? Was he such a great actor? Did we fail at checking his background adequately? So many things to ponder."

Aaisaheb patted Shivaji Raje's back, but her next words were not those of a consoling mother but an experienced, steely Queen. "If we want to continue to expand our boundaries, we need to answer those hard questions and plug all the loopholes in our security." She sighed and stood up. "On a lighter note, Prajakta and her gang always manage to help us in some way; things have an uncanny way of working out for the better when they get involved!"

The guards were surprised by the throaty laughter emerging from the Queen Mother's chambers.

"Yes, Mother, but in such a tortuous and twisted way, like a game of snakes and ladders!" the King concluded.

Chapter 22

The howls of the wolves reverberated through the jungle, making the two men shiver even more than the cold rain did. It would be hot as hell in Raigad at this time, Ganpat thought before breaking out into wild, soundless laughter. Well, he was still in a sort of hell! His companion eyed him curiously, then continued looking around for any beasts that lurked close by. They were so close to their goal! Ahmed's friends would join them the next morning, and then they'd receive a hero's welcome in Bijapur.

"Are there many wolves in these forests?" Ganpat asked. He touched the small dagger at his waist to make sure it was there – he even slept with the sharp weapon – it was all he had left of Shubham.

"Some," came the terse reply, "but they're scared of the elephants that live here in larger numbers."

"Elephants!" Ganpat remembered the Mavalas mocking his nose and his name, and felt a wave of hot rage sweep over him. He never should have left Indore for that cursed state. The lure of money, of being the clothier to the Maratha King, of believing in Swarajya and in freedom from foreign rule – what a fool he had been! And then he had fallen in love with Sugandha, the milkmaid.

Ganpat allowed himself to forget where he was and smiled at the memory of his feisty wife – she of the loud voice and soft heart, who was a fervent devotee of Aaisaheb and Shivaji. She worshipped the very ground they walked on, and had moved to Raigad just to be closer to them. Ganpat had heard her first before he saw her; she'd been bawling someone out for short-changing her, then she saw him ogling her and proceeded to yell at him, too!

Like the waves that rose and fell, her temper cooled in a few seconds, and beaming, she offered him some jamuns. He decided then and there that this was the woman for him. How happy they had been in those days, and when Shubham, their son, was born, it was as if Ganpat had found all the treasure in the world. The orphan boy finally had a family of his own! Their lad had grown up into a handsome young man with unmatched fighting skills, and it seemed almost inevitable that Shivaji's Sardars would seek to train him for their army. Then, Ganpat's breath hitched; disaster had struck. His own wretched childhood had hardened his heart, but love had begun the thawing process, and having a family to belong to had broken down his defences and made him susceptible to pain. The martyrdom of his beloved Shubham in the Battle of Salher sounded the death knell for his family too; his wife died of shock, and he was left reeling. Everything vanished in a trice, like an elaborate sandcastle levelled by the high tide.

After that, Ganpat continued to astound people with his exquisitely skillful work, but he was only a shell of a man. In the beginning, he was numb – a walking, breathing body going about his daily chores by default. Then, the grief set in, and finally, a small ember of rage flickered – rage for the cause his precious son died for, and rage for the man who sent him there, while he watched from the secure ramparts of his home. Ganpat was consumed by anger, and began to hate everything about Shivaji and his bloody Swarajya. And, when he heard that the King had the audacity to crown himself as Chhatrapati, Ganpat just couldn't take it anymore. His muttered ramblings must have been noticed, because out of the blue, one misty morning, Ahmed entered his life.

Well, his time at the Maratha's court was finally done. Their plan may not have succeeded in totality, but they had achieved what they set out to do – stop the Coronation, and turn the people against their beloved King. Ahmed was a master strategist, Ganpat thought. He was so convincing that the listener firmly believed it was his own idea. Their original plan to steal the Bhavani had not been practical because of the sword's weight and the impossibility of hiding it. Whatever his faults, Ganpat marvelled at the strength of the diminutive-looking Maratha King.

"Do you think they must have found the boy by now?" He felt a qualm at the thought of that child in the abandoned, dark dungeon. Why had that pesky boy turned up in his workshop?

Ahmed let out an evil chuckle. "One of the guards was walking in the direction of the dungeons; I told him I saw a boy going off alone towards Takmak Tok, and the fellow turned around and headed there instead. They will now spend the whole night searching there; a few of those bloody Marathas will fall off the cliffs!"

The howling of the wolves seemed to grow in intensity, and then suddenly they fell silent. The abrupt hush was somehow even scarier than the din they had been making. Ahmed cocked his head and said, "Did you hear that?"

"What?" Ganpat asked, and then, before they could blink, men wrapped in black shawls, armed with spears and swords, surrounded them.

"The Marathas!" Ahmed gasped.

Ganpat closed his eyes. It was all over. He gave the warriors a bitter smile. *I could not even do this right.* He burst into loud laughter, shocking his captors.

***

"Aaisaheb!" Rama burst into the kitchen where the Queen Mother was supervising the besan being roasted.

"What is it, Rama? *Aga, aga,* stay away from that pot, your *padar* will catch fire!"

Rama beamed at her, "The thieves have been caught!"

The Queen Mother handed the ladle to the cook and whispered, "You mean…?" She widened her eyes and glanced around, then led Rama to one side. "They have recovered the jewels?"

"Yes, all 13 of them!" Rama did a little dance. "They are heading back and will be home soon."

Aaisaheb motioned for the cook to bring over a little of the steaming-hot mixture of besan and sugar. She blew on it and offered a bit to Rama, "May you always bring such sweet news for our Kingdom and our people!"

Prajakta and the children hugged each other and screamed for joy. The Bhavani Talwar would be whole now, and the Coronation would go on as planned. All was well with the world!

"But did you find out how he did it?" Sarjya couldn't quite get the mystery out of his mind.

Tukoji's delighted expression faded, "Ganpat wasn't very cooperative in the beginning, but finally he admitted that he was fitting Raje for clothes for the Coronation when his co-conspirator Chandra came to give Raje the news that Soyarabaisaheb couldn't come in the evening as Shambhu Raje was still unwell. While she engaged Raje in conversation, Ganpat slipped into the weapons room and quickly removed the jewels."

"But he knew he would be frisked while going out!" Prajakta pointed out. "So he had to hide the stones."

"Yes, he had loosened one of the rocks in the meeting room the previous week, when he came for the first fitting, just enough to make the crevice you found. They had been very clever to think of a backup plan," a frowning Tukoji said, for the villain's cleverness only highlighted their own weak security.

"So, Ganpat hid the jewels there," Sarjya's eyes danced as he spoke, "and then pretended to have lost his thimble. Then, he returned four days later to take them and repair the crevice!"

"Wasn't he searched then?" Ganya's fearful tone was mingled with hatred for the tailor.

"The guard now admits he didn't check Ganpat the second time because he was only in the outer room, where there was nothing besides the bed."

Sarjya clapped his hand to his forehead. "Ah, that devious man! What an audacious plan he devised!"

Tukoji shook his head. "The tall, hefty fellow from Bijapur, Ahmed, was the mastermind; he brainwashed Ganpat, who was already eager to seek revenge on our King. Ganpat's rage and hatred for Shivaji were fertile soil for the poisonous words of the Bijapuri who concocted the whole scheme. He was the one who tempted Chandra with silver anklets and the promise of gold earrings, and even marriage. He pretended he was a nobleman at the Court of the Shindes and knew Ganpat since childhood at Indore."

"Will Chandra be punished too, Kaka?" Prajakta asked Tukoji.

"Yes, child. The staff close to Raje's family have to be scrupulously honest, so she will be jailed as an example to the rest to demonstrate what happens to those who betray their King."

"Ganpat and his friend are in irons too *na*, Kaka?" Ganya was still worried.

Tukoji looked at the boy's drawn face and smiled. "Don't worry, they will never see the light of day again!" Turning to the rest of the children, he pulled out something from his waistband; it was an ornate dagger. Tukoji held it out to Sopan and said, "I'd like to gift this to you. It was made for my brother Veeraji, and he always carried it with him. His soldiers adored him; he was a man's man, unlike….ahem… I'd like you to have it; I thought you would appreciate the extra-sharp blade and the detailed carving on the grip. After all, what would an administrator like me do with it?"

Sopan's jaw dropped. He gave Tukoji a sheepish smile and accepted the dagger. How wrong they had been about the man!

The children's excitement quickly died down as they were left to themselves over the next few hours.

"I'm bored!" Sarjya pouted. "No one has come to talk to us. Is this their way of saying we should go back home?"

Kaloo jumped out of the restless boy's lap and into Ganya's. "I'm hungry!" Ganya said.

"Again?" the three groaned.

"Why are you eating so much?" Sarjya put it bluntly, but it was a question they all wanted to know the answer to.

Ganya gulped, conscious of their eyes on him. "I…I don't know," he said. "These last few months, I couldn't bear the touch of my clothes on me – perhaps because the village boys thought my choice of clothing was strange, and they hooted whenever I passed them. I couldn't bear to even look at my reflection in the river water when I'd wash up. I felt fat and ugly – a source of entertainment and mockery. Eating would make things worse; I'd feel horrible as the food went down my throat, almost as I could feel it making me fatter and funnier. I used to throw up after most meals. Aai and Baba even asked Naik Kaka for medicines."

The boy sat in silence, unable to meet their eyes. Kaloo licked his face, making him giggle. "I wanted to become invisible – in the way I dressed, and in my body size."

"And so you became quieter and stopped imitating people and animals." Prajakta's eyes brimmed with tears.

Ganya nodded, "You all are so confident, so sure of what you want to do. Even if someone laughs at you, you don't bother too much. I felt alone, especially after Sarjya went to Sangamner and…"

Sarjya jumped up to hug his friend tightly and said, "You silly boy! Why didn't you tell me all this? I will always stand by your side, whether you wear grey or orange, whether you keep quiet or mimic a tiger!"

Sopan and Prajakta nodded, "Listen only to those who care for you because they will always love you just as you are."

***

A cough from the doorway alerted them to Rama's presence; she stood there for a while, teary-eyed, then smiled at them all. "It warms my heart to see all of you together. Your friendship is an example to everyone!" She hugged Ganya, who blushed. "What should I bring for you now, my hero? *Besan laadoo* or *kheer*?"

Once their laughter died down, she beamed, her body vibrating with excitement. "I have some news for you. Raje and Aaisaheb want you to stay on for the Coronation!" She raised her palm at their gasps and exclamations, then added, "But wait, there's more… the headman of your village, Maloji Naik, has been invited with his family, and so have all your parents!"

Sarjya's face shone with pride. "Our Aai and Baba will come here? This is a dream come true!"

"What's more, Aaisaheb plans to ask one of the tailors to take Ganya under his wing, with his parents' permission, of course. Who knows, in a few years, he may be surrounded by the richest jewels and silks and brocades, and may become the clothier to a Royal Family even!" Rama turned to Ganya and said, "Only if you want to."

"I want, I want!" Ganya blurted out, beaming from ear to ear.

Chapter 23

6th June, 1674

The much-awaited day had finally dawned. The preliminary rituals had been concluded, and the anointing ceremony or Rajyabhishek had been performed under Pandit Gagabhatt's supervision. Though it was very early in the morning, the Grand Hall was already packed with a hundred thousand excited guests. Eyes shining, Ganya nudged Prajakta when Shivaji Raje entered; the King's clothes, turban and jewels were a sight to behold, but it was the Bhavani Talwar that the children were looking at. The sight of the magnificent sword at the King's waist made them gasp, tear up, and then beam with pride at their role in getting it there. Their parents were by their side, nervous and uncomfortable in their hurriedly stitched clothes. Hanu Kaka especially kept plucking at his silk kurta, wondering when he would use it later. Probably at Sopan's wedding, he smiled.

Shivaji Raje slowly ascended to the throne, the final step in ensuring formal recognition of his kingdom. After vowing to govern and protect his people justly, he was seated on the glorious throne, after which Gagabhatt held the royal umbrella over his head and proclaimed,

"Maharaj, Sinhassanadheeshwar, Kshatriya kulawatouns, Maharajadhiraj, Raja Shiv Chhatrapati yancha vijay aso!"

Victory to the great King, ruler of the throne, pride of the Kshtriya clan, emperors of emperors, the great and noble King, Emperor Shivaji!

The assembled people erupted in joy, showering their newly crowned King with flowers and grains of rice. The sound of trumpets filled the hall, and cannons boomed from the ramparts, announcing to the world that the Marathi people would not bow before any other – they finally had their own King!

Sarjya skipped ahead of his overwhelmed parents, proudly showing them around the fort. His excited chatter came to an unexpected halt at the sight of Tukoji standing there with a young man. Prajakta's brows knitted. Where had she seen the man before?

"This is Surya, Raje's…no, no Chhatrapati's special officer," Tukoji said.

Prajakta remembered the cheerful young man she had met in Sangamner; it was the spy! She looked at the man curiously. Wasn't he too young for such a serious responsibility?

Tukoji addressed Sarjya, "I mentioned you to Surya – all your stealthy creeping about the fort, and listening in on all the conversations you shouldn't, and," he smiled, adding, "and how much you love your King! He wanted to meet you and maybe give you a few tips."

Prajakta turned to her brother and giggled at his reaction; it was the first time she had seen him unable to form words! He walked off with Surya, and the two moved to a corner to chat. A confused Aai asked, "Who is that man, *ga*? And why is Sarjya looking thunderstruck?"

"I will tell you everything in detail when we get back home," Prajakta's eyes met Baba's, and she smiled. She had a secret of her own to tell them all – Rama had praised her healing skills to the Queen Mother, who had then asked if she would return to the fort in a few weeks. Aaisaheb wanted Prajakta to live there for some months and decide whether she'd like to be a special assistant to the Royal Family. "Your knowledge of herbs and quick thinking is much required in our community. Even if you decide to go back to Naikwadi, you could train someone here in your skills," she had said. Prajakta was thrilled at the opportunity to be useful to her King and his family; no one would scoff at her here for not being like the other girls. Perhaps, being around Rama would also help ease her way into womanhood, and maybe marriage too – after many, many years of course!

Hanumanta rubbed his bald pate in amazement. Sopan had led him to the royal armoury, where the two had spent hours marvelling at the swords, shields and cannons. Moropant Pingale himself had thanked Sopan's father for the excellent quality of the blades he was fashioning for their new swords. "Your contribution to our war effort is truly appreciated! Maharaj has asked me to tell you how grateful he is," the Chief Minister had said. The blacksmith looked at his son, as if in a daze. He could never have dreamed that one day, his King would know his name! He grabbed Sopan's hand and held it tightly. This gang of friends was something special for sure. Who knew what they would do next!